This book should be returned to any branch of the
Lancashire County Library on or before the date shown

1 7 JUL 2015	1 7 JUL 2021	- 3 JAN 2019
1 1 AUG 2015		
0 4 JUN 2016		

1 0 SEP 2016		DEC 2020
2 3 JUN 2017		
3 0 APR 2019		

Lancashire County Library
Bowran Street
Preston PR1 2UX

Lancashire
County Council

www.lancashire.gov.uk/libraries

LL1(A)

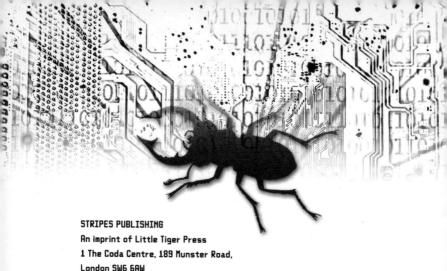

STRIPES PUBLISHING
An imprint of Little Tiger Press
1 The Coda Centre, 189 Munster Road,
London SW6 6AW

A paperback original
First published in Great Britain in 2015

Text copyright © Simon Cheshire, 2015
Cover illustration copyright © Adrian Chesterman, 2015
Cover background and inside imagery courtesy of www.shutterstock.com

ISBN: 978-1-84715-611-2

Printed and bound in the UK.

10 9 8 7 6 5 4 3 2 1

SWARM
TARGET SILVERCLAW

SIMON CHESHIRE

Stripes

SWARM

DEPARTMENT OF
MICRO-ROBOTIC INTELLIGENCE

SPECIALISTS IN NANOTECHNOLOGY AMD BIOMIMICRY

HEAD OF DEPARTMENT
Beatrice Maynard: Code name QUEEN BEE

HUMAN OPERATIVES

Prof. Thomas Miller: TECHNICIAN
Alfred Berners: PROGRAMMER
Simon Turing: DATA ANALYST

SWARM OPERATIVES

WIDOW

DIVISION: Spider
LENGTH: 1.5 cm
WEIGHT: 1 gram
FEATURES:
- 360º vision and recording function
- Produces silk threads and webs stronger than steel
- Extremely venomous bite
- Can walk on any surface – horizontal, vertical or upside down

CHOPPER

DIVISION: Dragonfly
LENGTH: 12 cm
WEIGHT: 0.8 grams
FEATURES:
- Telescopic vision with zoom, scanning and recording functions
- Night vision and thermal imaging abilities
- High-speed flight with super control and rapid directional change

NERO

DIVISION: Scorpion
LENGTH: 12 cm
WEIGHT: 30 grams
FEATURES:
- Strong, impact-resistant exoskeleton
- Pincers to grab and hold, with high dexterity
- Venomous sting in tail
- Capable of high-speed attack movements

SABRE

DIVISION: Mosquito
LENGTH: 2 cm
WEIGHT: 2.5 milligrams
FEATURES:
- Long proboscis (mouthparts) for extracting DNA and injecting tracking technology and liquids to cause paralysis or memory loss
- Specialist in stealth movement without detection
- Capable of recording low frequency, low-volume sound

HERCULES

DIVISION: Stag beetle
LENGTH: 5 cm
WEIGHT: 50 grams
FEATURES:
- Extra-tough membrane on wing shells to withstand extreme force and pressure
- Serrated claw for sawing through any material
- Can lay surveillance 'eggs' for tracking and data analysis

MORPH

DIVISION: Centipede
LENGTH: 5 cm (10 cm when fully extended)
WEIGHT: 100 milligrams
FEATURES:
- Flexible, gelatinous body with super-strong grip
- Ability to dig and burrow
- Laser-mapping sensory functions

SIRENA

DIVISION: Butterfly
LENGTH: 7 cm
WEIGHT: 0.3 grams
FEATURES:
- Uses beauty rather than stealth for protection
- Expert in reconnaissance missions – can gather environmental data through high-sensitivity antennae

CHAPTER ONE

The large grandfather clock chimed eleven. Although it was late in the evening, the fifth-floor hallway of the UK's Ministry of Defence building was brightly lit.

The chimes were all that could be heard in the hallway. A thick carpet allowed a tall figure, carrying a large suitcase, to move without a sound. The figure's smart polished shoes moved past the clock, walking slowly towards a closed door a little further along the corridor.

Behind that door was an expensively furnished office. Sir Godfrey Kite, Secretary of

State for Defence, sat at a wide desk, checking through some official papers. Open in front of him was a bright red despatch box, one of the official cases used by British ministers to carry documents. The only light in the room was the white glow from a reading lamp, shining on the desk's surface. Beyond this pool of light, the office was dark and shadowy.

Sir Godfrey was a short, middle-aged man with grey hair and a square jaw. He wore a pair of half-moon spectacles perched on his nose. He sat back, stretched and yawned, then glanced at his chunky wristwatch.

"Is that really the time?" he muttered quietly to himself. He'd been concentrating so hard on his work, he hadn't even noticed the chiming of the grandfather clock.

He placed his spectacles on the desk and rubbed his eyes. He checked through some of the papers in front of him and dropped them back into his despatch box. He'd deal with them in the morning, he decided. He was too tired to give them proper attention now.

He paused. He thought he'd heard... What

was that? It sounded like someone had brushed against the outside of his door.

He sat still and silent for a moment, then called out, "Is that you, Havelock? I thought everyone had gone home hours ago!"

Silence.

After a few seconds, Sir Godfrey shook his head and smiled to himself. "I need a good night's sleep, that's all," he mumbled.

There it was again! A rustling sound, as if someone was listening at his door. There was no mistaking it this time.

"Who's there?" barked Sir Godfrey. He flushed with anger. "I'm in no mood for pranks, I warn you! Havelock, if you think this is—"

He stopped mid-sentence. He shielded the light from the lamp with a hand and peered into the gloom.

The handle of the door was turning, very slowly.

For a moment, Sir Godfrey felt a flash of fear. Then his anger returned. "Right! That's quite enough of this!"

He jumped to his feet, marched to the door and flung it wide open. The figure carrying the large suitcase stood absolutely still in the doorway.

Sir Godfrey took a step back, and then another. His eyes widened. His mind struggled to make sense of what he was seeing.

"W-what's going on?" he cried in a trembling voice. "If this is a joke, it's in very poor taste!"

The figure remained still and silent.

Sir Godfrey backed away, his eyes fixed on the stranger, and collided with his desk. The desk lamp shuddered momentarily, then toppled over. A bright glare now shone directly at the mysterious figure.

"O-oh my…" stammered Sir Godfrey. "W-who are you?"

The figure took a step forward. He had the face of Sir Godfrey Kite, Secretary of State for Defence.

"Who are you?" demanded the real Sir Godfrey loudly.

"Surely you know your own reflection?" said the stranger. He had Sir Godfrey's voice, too. He was even wearing an identical suit.

"I'm going mad!" cried Sir Godfrey. His eyes bulged and sweat broke out on his forehead. "I'm going completely mad!"

"No," smiled the stranger. "You're going to sleep."

He raised his hand and fired a tiny dart from a small device. It hit Sir Godfrey in the neck and the politician slowly crumpled to the floor, unconscious.

The fake Sir Godfrey went to work. He didn't bother shutting the office door, because he knew for certain that there was nobody else in the building except the two security guards at the main entrance. He sat at the desk, picked up the lamp and set it back in its place, then sorted through the papers in the despatch box, locating the one he'd come for. It was marked "Top Secret".

He picked up the landline phone and tapped in a number from the secret document. The call was answered almost immediately.

"Call location confirmed," said the government officer at the other end. "Ministry of Defence, London. Please establish ID."

"This is Sir Godfrey Kite," said the imposter.

There was a short pause. "Voice-print ID confirmed," said the officer.

The imposter read a code number from the secret document. "Shipment AE-X-4567-beta is to be re-routed. It will now be picked up by aircraft at Location 11-88 on the north-west coast."

"Are you sure, sir?"

"Of course I'm sure!"

"Sorry, sir, but my records show that shipment is a consignment of weaponry. It's not usual for—"

"This is a security measure," interrupted the imposter. "A last-minute, unannounced change to fool the terrorists!"

"Of course, sir," spluttered the officer.

"See to it," said the imposter. Without waiting for a reply, he put down the phone.

He slipped a smartphone from his jacket pocket and sent a text:

Platinum 1 to Silverclaw.
Secretary of State for Defence
has been acquired. Substitute
made. Shipment of weapons
re-routed, as ordered.

The imposter stood up and opened the large suitcase he'd brought with him. He placed the unconscious Sir Godfrey into it, in a curled-up position, and locked it. He glanced around the office to check that everything looked normal, then picked up the case and walked away down the hall. He carried the suitcase as if it was no heavier than when it had been empty.

Downstairs at the main entrance, one of the guards came out of the small security station to meet him.

"Did you get what you needed, sir?" said the guard.

The imposter tapped the suitcase. "I did indeed, thank you. So many papers! I know I ought to use the despatch boxes, but one big case is so much easier to manage."

"I quite understand, sir," smiled the guard. "Oh, by the way…"

"Yes?"

"When you came in, sir, half an hour ago. When I said I thought you were still up in your office, sir…"

"Yes?"

"The thing is, sir, we hadn't checked you out of the building. According to the log, you hadn't left, but now we've logged you as coming in and going again, when we didn't know you'd gone in the first place, if you see what I mean?"

The imposter shrugged. "Well, as you can see, I must have left earlier, or I couldn't have returned now, could I?" He laughed, and the guard chuckled along with him.

"It's just that we have to stick to the rules, sir," said the guard, squirming slightly, "and these days one tiny security slip up can get people like me into a whole world of trouble, sir."

The imposter leaned closer to the guard and spoke in a whisper. "Mistakes happen, old chap. I tell you what, you say nothing about me not using the proper despatch boxes, and I won't say anything about the log slip up, how's that? If anyone gives you any trouble, send them to me. I'll back you up."

The guard gave him a wobbly grin. "That's very good of you, sir, really."

"No problem. Now, could you call my car round? I'll go straight to my flat."

"Right away!" smiled the guard.

A few moments later, a sleek black ministerial car glided to a halt outside the gate. The imposter got into the back, pulling the suitcase in beside him.

The car sped away into the night.

CHAPTER TWO

"8:58 a.m. Two minutes to bomb detonation. Move in!"

The electronic voice buzzed across an encrypted communications network. It was answered by six others. "Logged," said each of them. "I'm live!"

The scene outside the Palace of Westminster seemed totally normal. Streams of traffic crawled and honked along Westminster Bridge, past Big Ben and around Parliament Square. Hundreds of people crowded the streets; Londoners hurrying to work and tourists snapping selfies.

"Target ahead. Sensors at maximum sweep."

Nobody paid any attention to a large white van parked close to the Palace of Westminster, near the lawns of Abington Street Gardens. It was an old, rather rusty vehicle, with "D, G & I Plumbing Solutions Ltd" painted in large letters along the side beneath a smiling cartoon dog holding a sink plunger.

People walking by had no idea that the three men sitting on the front seats were heavily armed terrorists. Between them, they were keeping a close watch on the area around the van. In the compartment behind them, sealed off from normal electronic scans and the noses of sniffer dogs, were cardboard crates packed floor to ceiling. They contained enough concentrated explosive to reduce everything within a half-mile radius to rubble and dust. A trigger was held gingerly by the terrorist at the steering wheel.

The passers-by had no idea that this threat was about to be dealt with by a team of undercover agents unlike any other. The agents were closing in on the van.

"Ninety seconds until the prime minister's car

passes the van. Move in!"

"Scans show driver has a manual detonator. Proceed with caution!"

"Logged."

The seven undercover agents were micro-robots, each taking the outward form of a bug. Chopper the dragonfly circled the area, coordinating the mission and relaying instructions; Hercules the stag beetle flew at speed towards the van, carrying Nero the scorpion in his metal legs; Sabre the tiny mosquito flew beside them; Widow the spider swung across the road, from car bumper to car bumper, on thin web-wires; Morph the centipede scuttled up through a drain cover and approached the van from underneath; and high above them fluttered Sirena the butterfly, her ultra-sensitive probes scanning every detail of the activity below.

These robots were part of SWARM, an organization so secret that only a handful of people knew it existed. The robots' advanced brains processed data about the van, the terrorists inside it and everything nearby faster than any human could. Their circuits streamed information back to SWARM headquarters, hidden deep beneath the streets of London.

"Hercules, get Nero inside," transmitted Chopper. "Priority one: disable the bomb."

"OK," signalled Hercules the stag beetle.

"The correct response is 'logged'," tutted Nero as he scurried to one side of the van.

Hercules landed on its roof and quickly cut a small, perfectly round hole in the metal surface using the sharp pincer that jutted forward from his toughened exoskeleton.

Inside the van, the driver held up a hand for silence. "Shh! Can you hear something? It sounds like scratching…"

All three terrorists were in a state of nervous dread.

"What?" cried another. "No, I can't! Keep watching what's going on outside!"

All three had machine guns hidden just out of view. The third man gripped his gun tightly to stop his hands from shaking. "The prime minister's car will be here any minute…" he muttered to himself. "This is it…"

"Fifty-eight seconds and counting," signalled

Chopper. "Sirena, what's Sabre's best route in?"

"Both windows firmly shut," reported Sirena, her sensors analyzing everything from the chemical composition of the glass to the body temperature of the three terrorists. "He needs to go up through the air vents."

"Logged," said Sabre. Darting in swift, buzzing movements like a real mosquito, he flew through the grille at the front of the van and along the inside surface of the bonnet.

"Morph, Widow," said Chopper. "Disable the van."

"Logged."

Widow whipped around the van's exhaust pipe and swung beneath the wheel arch. She leaped from wheel to wheel, binding them into fixed positions with threads stronger than steel cable. If the terrorists tried to move the van, the wheels would be completely immobilized, thanks to Widow's web.

Meanwhile, Morph the centipede flattened his gelatinous body until he was thin enough to slip inside the van's engine. He curled around whatever moving parts he could find and squeezed them until they cracked.

"We'd better hurry," he said. "If they suspect they're being attacked they'll detonate the bomb early."

"Forty seconds," said Chopper.

"Scanning…" said Sirena. "They're watching the street. Sabre, you're safe to proceed."

"Logged," said Sabre.

He darted out of one of the air vents set into the van's dashboard. Before any of the terrorists had time to notice a little insect buzzing around their heads, Sabre had loaded a microscopic pellet into his needle-like proboscis. He shot forward and injected it into the neck of the terrorist holding the bomb's detonator.

"Stinger delivered," he said.

The man suddenly let out a squeal and lurched upright.

"What is it?" cried the man sitting next to him.

Sabre buzzed through a semicircle in mid-air and injected a sting behind the second man's ear. He too yelped. Then both of them slumped over.

The third terrorist cried out in alarm. He looked outside in a panic, wondering what was going on.

"Thirty seconds," said Chopper.

By now, Nero had crawled in through the hole in the roof and was scuttling upside down, close to the windscreen.

"Better knock this one out fast," he transmitted. "Humans act in irrational ways when scared."

Sabre zipped past the two unconscious terrorists. The third was reaching out for the timer, to set off the bomb, when Sabre swooped down and stung the back of the man's hand. He snatched it back, yelling in pain. Then he twitched violently in his seat and drooped against the windscreen, his face squashed into an ugly twist against the glass.

"I've detected a booby trap!" said Sirena. "A second detonator deep inside the van's rear compartment. It was set off when Hercules cut his way in. Timer is at twenty-three … twenty-two seconds. Transmitting coordinates."

"Nero, you have twenty seconds," said Chopper calmly.

Without a word, Nero the scorpion scurried around the packing boxes in the rear of the van until he reached the timer. Thin fibre-optic probes shot out of his pincers and dug into the timer's electronic mechanism.

"Ten seconds," said Chopper.

The probes tested the timer's circuits. The mathematical subroutines in Nero's programming worked out how to send a stop signal into the bomb without triggering any more traps or anti-tampering devices.

The numbers on the front of the timer went haywire. For a second or two, they blinked and scrambled, then the timer switched itself off.

"Bomb deactivated," said Nero. "Seven seconds to spare. It was quite a simple machine, in the end. Those terrorists were nowhere near as clever as they thought they were."

"Hive 1 to SWARM HQ," transmitted Chopper. "Mission accomplished."

"This is SWARM HQ," came a voice on the communications system. It was Beatrice Maynard, codenamed Queen Bee, the human leader of SWARM. "Excellent work."

"The terrorists are ready for the authorities," said Chopper. "The bomb has been disarmed."

"Acknowledged," said Queen Bee. "Now get

out of there. I'll send our human agents to clean up and get everything handed over to MI5."

"It hardly seems fair that we can't take any credit," said Hercules.

"If we took credit for our missions," said Nero, "we couldn't operate in secret, could we?"

The SWARM robots regrouped fifteen metres above the ground, the heavy-duty stag beetle, Hercules, carrying Nero with his legs and Widow on his back. Morph held on tightly to Chopper.

Moving in a spaced-out formation, they flew in a wide curve, close to the huge, cathedral-like shape of the Palace of Westminster. They were small enough to be almost invisible from ground level.

"Now that we have successfully completed several missions since we were first activated," said Morph, "I'm beginning to understand why humans say they're happy at times like this. My circuits acknowledge that our task is complete, and it registers as a positive binary sequence in my central processor."

"How inconvenient. Perhaps there's a fault in your programming," said Nero.

"Our next task is here already," said Sirena.

"We have nothing coming through from Queen Bee," said Chopper.

"No," said Sirena, "but something is coming through on my sensor grid. I'm picking up some odd signals. Scanning… They're coming from inside the Palace of Westminster."

"What's odd about them?" said Hercules.

"Analyzing…" said Sirena. "Results inconclusive. It's some sort of strange electromagnetic pulse. Our link-ups to official data tells me there shouldn't be anything like that in there. Something must be wrong."

"Can you ID the source?" said Chopper.

"Negative," said Sirena. "I'd need to get closer. The pulses are similar to the signals we use to transmit information. Much lower band, but similar."

"Is anyone from SWARM in the building right now?" said Hercules. "Perhaps Professor Miller is demonstrating our systems to someone in the government?"

Nero remotely hacked into a series of databases, online diaries and security systems, then cross-referenced everything he found. In exactly 1.93 seconds, he concluded: "There's nobody in the Palace of Westminster this morning who's even heard of SWARM. None of the humans we know are present."

"Hive 1 to SWARM HQ," transmitted Chopper.

"HQ here, proceed," said Queen Bee.

Chopper sent Sirena's scans back to base. "Stand by, Hive 1," said Queen Bee. There was a soft beep on the network.

"We should investigate immediately," said Sabre.

"Not without clearance from Queen Bee," said Chopper. "We're designed to act independently, but not to break the rules."

Queen Bee came back online. "I've spoken to Simon and Alfred here in the lab. Proceed with extreme caution. Repeat, extreme caution. We don't have official permission to conduct an investigation inside the Palace of Westminster, and getting permission would take time that we might not have. Those signals could switch off at any moment."

"We'll observe and scan only," said Chopper.

"Take extra care not to trip their alarms," said Queen Bee. "The World Leaders' Security Conference takes place at the end of the week, so they're on red alert."

"I've downloaded a full readout of the security systems," said Nero. "Getting in will be easy."

"Make sure it is," said Queen Bee. "If any of you are caught or identified as robots, SWARM could be shut down. Report back as soon as you have something. Queen Bee out."

It took the SWARM robots less than five minutes to work their way around the series of motion detectors, X-ray scanners and steel reinforcements that protected the Palace of Westminster. They slipped through tiny gaps, burrowed into heating and electrical conduits, and hitched rides on passing shoes and coats.

As they moved through the building, the signals Sirena was picking up were getting steadily clearer. The seven robots fanned out across the eastern side of the building, staying in the shadows, combining their sensor data to help pinpoint the source.

Seven minutes and twenty-two seconds after

the signal was first detected, the SWARM robots found themselves in an air duct, high up in the main chamber of the House of Commons. Chopper, whose optical circuits were the most powerful, looked out across the floor of the House from behind an old-fashioned metal grate. The others tapped into his visual data stream.

MPs sat on long benches that ran down both sides of the huge chamber. Above them, behind bulletproof glass, was the gallery where journalists and members of the public watched the debates taking place below.

"Location pinpointed," said Sirena. "Signals originate at bearing 342.5, range 16.9 metres."

Chopper's eyes zoomed in. The SWARM team saw a short, middle-aged man sitting on the front bench on the government's side of the House.

"Accessing remote databases," said Nero the scorpion. "Positive ID. That is Sir Godfrey Kite, Secretary of State for Defence."

"What's generating those signals?" said Morph. "Is he armed?"

"If he is," said Sabre, "we'll have to disable the weapon at once, even if we risk getting caught."

"He isn't armed," said Sirena. "Now we're close enough, I can scan him at maximum intensity. There's a strange reflective layer beneath his skin. Any standard X-ray or security equipment would be fooled into seeing him as a normal human being, but I can probe beyond that."

"Results?" said Chopper.

"It's very puzzling," said Sirena. "But there can be no doubt. Sir Godfrey Kite is a robot."

CHAPTER THREE

At that same moment, in a remote part of Scotland, events in the House of Commons were being closely monitored.

"Sensor probe detected," said a flat, mechanical voice.

"Specify," came a female voice in reply. It was clear from the intonation the speaker was human.

"Unable to identify. Location within twenty metres of our unit."

"Zoom in!"

Smooth, humanoid hands moved across a control panel. Although this machine was similar to the Sir Godfrey Kite robot in London, this one wasn't required to pass as a human, so it had no face. Its external appearance was basic and unformed, with a small round speaker instead of a mouth. The panel it was sitting at formed part of a large room filled with screens and machinery. Identical faceless robots worked at other controls. The room was lit only by the glow of displays and the flashing coloured lights on the machines.

"Acknowledged. Attempting to focus." The hands tapped a touchscreen display.

The human giving the orders got up from her tall, curved chair and walked over to the control panel. There was a whirring sound as she moved. Her right leg and right arm were bio-mechanical replacements. The right-hand side of her head was scattered with metallic patches and implants. A dark oval lens took the place of her right eye.

She stabbed at a series of controls. "It may be a routine sensor sweep ... or perhaps it's something to do with the Security Conference." She spoke into a microphone that was connected to the control panel on a long flexible stalk. "Silverclaw to Platinum 1, this is Gold Leader."

SWARM

The voice of Sir Godfrey Kite's duplicate, transmitted from inside its electronic brain without any outward sign, came from a nearby speaker. "Acknowledged, Silverclaw. This is Platinum 1."

"There's unusual sensor activity close to you. Scan and monitor."

"Acknowledged. Powering up scan software."

SWARM watched as Sir Godfrey's duplicate began to look about. As the MPs surrounding him debated noisily, his head turned slowly this way and that.

"There's computer-processing activity starting up inside that robot," said Sirena.

"I'm picking it up, too," said Nero. "Analyzing… It seems to be a basic set of scanning subroutines. Quite powerful, but not very focused. By the way, that's not a robot."

"But it's a machine, like us," said Hercules.

"As it's built in human form," said Nero, "then strictly speaking it's an android. We are robots. That is an android."

"Whatever it is, it's looking directly this way!" said Morph. "What if it's seen us?"

Chopper's lenses zoomed in closer. The android's eyes were examining the area around the air duct in which the SWARM robots were hiding.

In the Silverclaw control room, Gold Leader watched as graphs on several of the screens in front of her began to spike. The android beside her made adjustments to the controls.

"There's something in that area," muttered Gold Leader. "Something in the walls?" She turned to the android. "Can you ID it?"

"Readings indicate ultra-high frequencies," said the android flatly. "Most are outside our decoding range."

"Very advanced technology, then," said Gold Leader.

"Readings show a cluster of seven small objects, but further data cannot be obtained without moving Platinum 1 closer."

"We can't have our Sir Godfrey walking about examining the walls," said Gold Leader. "He must act normally at all times, otherwise he might raise suspicions. Continue to monitor."

"Acknowledged."

At that moment, a communicator built into the control panel beeped. Gold Leader switched it on. Her heart – half organic, half plastic – began to race with fear when she heard the low voice at the other end of the line. She recognized the voice as her only contact with the secret international crime syndicate funding the Silverclaw project. She didn't even know the organization's name. Her masters required frequent reports and didn't tolerate mistakes.

"Your systems show odd activity in London," said the voice. "Explain."

Gold Leader cleared her throat nervously. "There's no problem, sir. We located a sensor sweep. It's of an unknown type, but with the World Leaders' Security Conference in a matter of days, it's almost certainly routine. Our unit cannot have been identified as an android. The clumsy security forces there would have charged in and dragged it away if that was the case. All our units are designed to reflect normal bio-signatures."

The voice didn't answer for a moment. "You have arranged weaponry for the main strike?"

"Yes, sir. Platinum 1 re-routed a large consignment last night. Enough to arm every android we've built, and more. Delivery will take place soon."

Seconds ticked by. "Very well. We're watching Silverclaw's progress closely, Gold Leader. More than one recent effort has failed, including the Firestorm project. Success means rewards. Failure means punishment."

Gold Leader struggled to keep her voice steady. "I understand, sir. There'll be no failure."

The communicator switched itself off.

Gold Leader took a deep breath. The call had rattled her nerves. "Boost the power!" she barked at the android. "Get me more data on what's been scanning that building!"

"Acknowledged," said the android calmly.

"Why wasn't I told about these scanners?" cried Gold Leader. "Has the syndicate's mole inside MI5 been hiding things from me?"

She turned to one of the other androids, who was watching a screen that flowed with numbers. "Is our MI5 mole still under arrest?"

"Affirmative," said the android. "Since his cover was blown, MI5 have been questioning him at a safe house in London."

"Then it's time we set him free," said Gold Leader. "Send a squad to get him out. I want him here, with me. There must be information he hasn't given us... I'll wring it out of him!"

She turned back to the android monitoring the Sir Godfrey duplicate. "We can't get Sir Godfrey searching, but we can pull in more units. Who have we got near the Palace of Westminster?"

"Platinum 2 and Platinum 3 have replaced two journalists," replied the android. "Platinum 4 has replaced one of the building's cleaning staff. All three are within nine hundred metres and can gain entry to relevant areas."

"Send them in. And boost power to maximum. I want results!"

In London, Chopper had sent an update back to SWARM HQ. Professor Miller, SWARM's Chief Technician, tapped into the robots' communications network.

"You've uncovered a major threat!" he said. "That android could be part of—"

"Power levels rising!" interrupted Nero. "The android is boosting its scanning patterns."

"Could it ID us?" asked Morph.

"It definitely knows we're paying attention to it," said Sabre. "Should we attack, while we still have the element of surprise?"

"Negative," said Chopper. "Everyone, reduce output!"

All seven robots immediately powered down as many of their systems as possible. Only Chopper kept a low-band connection to HQ switched on and relayed it to the others.

"Good," said Professor Miller. "Stay at very low power levels and you should be beyond the android's ability to find you."

"What if it's already gathered data on us?" said Morph. "It could transmit SWARM secrets to whoever's controlling it."

"It's very unlikely that it's worked out who, or what, you are," said the professor. "At best, it would have simply seen seven small objects, and many different things might register as that. Your scans show that it's a highly sophisticated machine, but it doesn't have the kind of advanced systems available to SWARM. For one thing, it won't have realized we've identified it as an android. Only next-generation remote probes like Sirena's could have scanned it closely enough to discover the truth. We'll run further breakdowns on the information you've sent us," said the professor. "HQ out." There was a beep on the communications network.

The SWARM micro-robots watched the Sir Godfrey android look away again, returning its gaze to the parliamentary debate going on around it.

"What do we do now?" asked Morph. "We can't stay here like this. At such a low power setting, we can barely crawl at the speed of real bugs."

Nero allowed a small electrical charge to run through his data processors for a moment.

"Mathematical analysis shows that our best course of action is to split up. Once we're out of the android's immediate range, we can return to full power. Between us, we can keep a careful eye on the android's movements, making sure we don't arouse its suspicions. Then we can track it back to whoever controls it."

"What if it never leaves the Palace of Westminster?" said Morph. "We shouldn't really be in here at all, remember."

"I think we should follow Nero's plan," said Hercules. "We don't know where this android came from, and we don't know why it's here."

"Why would the humans want an android as one of their senior politicians?" said Morph. "Didn't any humans want the job?"

"I think you've reduced the power in your brain too far," said Nero. "This android must have replaced Sir Godfrey Kite."

"Recently, too," said Sabre. "The android looks very convincing, but humans would probably spot something wasn't quite right eventually."

"It took us a matter of minutes," said Nero.

"If the android has replaced a human as

Secretary of State for Defence," said Sirena, "what has happened to the real Sir Godfrey Kite? Where is he now?"

Through the robots' discussion, Widow stayed silent, as usual.

"Disconnect, scatter, then power-up and report in," said Chopper.

"Logged," replied the others.

Moving as quickly as their low-powered metal limbs would carry them, the SWARM agents spread out. They scurried into the rooms that surrounded the main House of Commons chamber. As soon as they were well out of range of the android, they switched their systems back to normal.

"Online," they reported, one after the other.

The moment each one was back on the network, they heard Sirena's voice making an urgent transmission:

"—hear me yet? Everyone? I've picked up more signals! There are three more androids entering the building with high-power scanners! Two are posing as journalists, the other as a cleaner. They must be hunting down the source of the scans

we made. In other words, they're after us! If they
get within range of any of us..."

"Understood, Sirena," transmitted Chopper.
"Emergency change of plan. Four androids pose
too much of a risk. Leave the building! Return to
SWARM HQ!"

"Logged," replied the others.

CHAPTER FOUR

In another part of the city, two men sat facing each other across a kitchen table. The kitchen was an ordinary one, in a plain-looking house on an unremarkable street, but it held a secret. This particular house had been modified with bulletproof windows and reinforced doors. It was a "safe house" used by the government – as a refuge for people in danger, or as somewhere for intelligence agents to keep a low profile. On some occasions it was used as a store for important items, away from prying eyes.

It was currently functioning as a kind of prison.

One of the men at the kitchen table was an MI5 section chief. The other was the prisoner – until recently an MI5 agent himself. He was a small, round man with a moustache. His lined face seemed to be set in a permanent sneer. His name was Morris Drake. He and SWARM were old enemies, even though Drake had never even heard of SWARM. The micro-robots had fought him – without his knowledge – during the Project Venom case, and he had finally been exposed as a traitor during the Code Name Firestorm operation.

The section chief slapped a file of official documents on to the table. "Are you going to talk to me today, Drake?"

"Are you going to cut me a deal and put me into a witness protection scheme instead of sending me to prison?"

The section chief sighed. "You know perfectly well, Drake, that any deal depends on what information you give us. Supply good intelligence on this –" he twirled his hand in mid-air – "mysterious criminal organization you keep hinting at, and then I'll see what I can do."

"You guarantee me protection, and then I'll supply the information," said Drake.

The section chief shut his eyes and let out a long, slow breath. "So you've been saying for weeks. But we need more. So far you've offered no proof that you're part of an international criminal syndicate. You won't even tell us this organization's name!"

"I don't know it," grinned Drake. "That's the beauty of the thing. Almost everyone who works for it has no idea who runs it, or how it's run."

"And yet you claim to know what they're planning? You know details of the evil schemes they're cooking up?"

Drake winked at him. "I know a lot more than they think I do."

"But you're not going to tell us what they're up to?" said the section chief.

Drake leaned forward across the table. "Not without guaranteed protection. If they ever … ever … got the slightest clue that I'd talked, they'd have me killed without a moment's thought."

Meanwhile, in the living room, one MI5 agent was monitoring the CCTV that covered the rear of the house and a second agent kept watch on the street from a bedroom window upstairs. He saw a large powerful car pull up on the opposite side of the street. A postman with a trolley appeared from the other direction. Not the regular postman, the agent noticed.

The driver of the car sat still and silent behind the wheel. The agent frowned slightly.

Back in the kitchen, the section chief was finding his conversation with Drake more irritating by the minute.

"I think you're just playing for time," he growled. "I don't think you really know anything. You're just stringing us along, so you can stay here with your own private bodyguard, instead of being slung into a prison cell where you belong."

Drake smiled. "Don't forget, I used to be one of you. I know all the tricks."

The section chief struggled to control his temper. He spoke slowly. "I want proof. And I want it now."

Upstairs, the agent on watch was growing nervous. The postman had walked straight past every other address in the street, but had now stopped in front of the safe house. He reached inside his trolley and took out a bundle of small square parcels wrapped in brown paper. The agent's heart thudded. Drawing a gun from inside his jacket, he headed for the stairs.

The driver of the car suddenly got out. He was dressed in grey workman's overalls, and carried a large roll of wallpaper under his arm.

Downstairs in the living room, the other MI5 agent heard a sharp, "Heads up! Out front!" come from upstairs. She looked up from her laptop and saw the postman standing a short distance back from the front of the house. She leaped to her feet, reaching for her revolver.

The postman raised one of the small parcels high above his head. Then he flung it at the front door of the safe house.

As it hit the door, it exploded, making the entire house shudder. The door was blown off its hinges and toppled flat into the hallway, leaving the entrance to the house wide open.

The agents on guard instantly dashed for the hallway, levelling their guns.

The postman and the decorator advanced

towards the smoking hole where the door had been. The postman lobbed a second parcel into the house. It detonated beside the stairs. The house shook again and the banister shattered into splinters of wood.

In the kitchen, the section chief also drew a gun. He aimed it squarely at Drake.

"Is this your doing?" he demanded.

"I'm afraid not," said Drake, with an icy calm.

The agent on duty downstairs rushed out into the hall. As the decorator walked swiftly towards him, she fired twice, but the bullets ricocheted off the man's chest and he didn't stop walking.

The decorator squeezed the roll of wallpaper he was carrying. A canister hidden inside it suddenly sent a jet of knock-out gas into the agent's face. She coughed, staggered and dropped to the floor.

The agent who'd been on watch upstairs saw what had happened and fired shot after shot at the two figures, who advanced, completely unaffected by the bullets. The decorator swung around and directed a blast of the gas at him and the agent fell back against the stairs.

In the kitchen, the section chief rose to his feet.

"Move a millimetre and you're dead!" he spat at Drake. He rushed into the living room, but the postman had got there before him. The android threw a parcel at the floor and the deafening explosion it caused tore an armchair to pieces and blew the section chief across the room. He slammed into a bookcase and collapsed into a heap, unconscious.

In the kitchen, Drake heard glass smash behind him. He whipped around and saw an android dressed as a gardener appearing through a broken window. He turned to run but the android grabbed both his arms from behind and gripped tightly. The postman and the decorator androids appeared in the kitchen doorway.

"I take it the Silverclaw operation is under way," said Drake, shifting uncomfortably in the vice-like hold of the android.

"Correct," said the postman. "You are to report to Gold Leader."

"Why? That wasn't part of the plan. I was only supposed to advise." Drake frowned.

"Gold Leader orders you to report."

Drake stared at the postman android. "I must

congratulate her. If I didn't know better, I'd think you were humans."

"We are standard Mercury units," said the postman. "More-advanced Platinum units are deployed in other areas of the mission."

"Very good," said Drake. "Now, can you tell this one to let me go? I'm on your side, you know! You don't have to—"

He was interrupted by a jet of knock-out gas. His head rocked from side to side for a second, then slumped back. The android who had been restraining him simply held him up at arm's length and all three walked quickly and quietly to the car. They bundled Drake on to the back seat, before getting in themselves.

The car sped away, as the wail of police sirens sounded in the distance.

At SWARM headquarters, the human personnel were gathered in the laboratory. The room was brightly lit and filled with a vast array of advanced electronic equipment. On one of the raised workbenches in the centre of the lab, the seven SWARM micro-robots were recharging in webs of circuits and wires, listening to the discussion as they regained power.

Beside them, SWARM's Data Analyst Simon Turing and Computer Programmer Alfred Berners were examining a 3D computer display showing a reconstructed visual of the Sir Godfrey android's head.

"This is brilliant work," Simon said quietly, not taking his eyes off the display. "They've managed to get the skin texture exactly right. You see this section here, Fred? If I zoom in a bit... There! Every hair follicle, every pore. Brilliant."

Alfred lifted his spectacles and screwed up his eyes to peer closely at the image. "Yes. Rather creepy. You can't tell it from real skin, can you?"

SWARM's leader, Queen Bee, was standing behind them. She gave a sharp, theatrical cough. "If we've finished admiring the handiwork, gentlemen, perhaps we could concentrate on mission details?"

"Ah, yes. Sorry Ms Maynard." Simon smiled.

Professor Miller was seated at a nearby

machine, using a microscope and mechanical arms to create miniature circuit boards. He gave Simon a disapproving glance.

"I've informed MI5 that there's a threat inside the Palace of Westminster," said Queen Bee. "They're doubling all patrols and checks. I haven't shared the full details of the situation with them because, as far as we know, only SWARM are capable of detecting these androids. It's up to SWARM, and SWARM alone, to deal with this problem."

"Couldn't MI5 simply arrest Sir Godfrey Kite?" said Simon. "Or rather, his duplicate?"

"Without knowing where these androids came from or what they're up to, that might make things worse," replied Queen Bee. "The arrest of a senior cabinet minister would be all over the news in minutes. What else do we know about the androids?"

"Examination of their data processing shows that they can't really think for themselves," said Alfred. "They act on instructions only."

"Do we know where these instructions are coming from?" said Queen Bee.

The electronic voice of Sirena came through a

speaker in the workbench. "Negative, Queen Bee. I scanned multiple wavebands, but the android's control transmissions were lost behind normal background electromagnetic interference."

"We think they're controlled using something very similar to mobile-phone data," said Simon. "It's almost impossible to pick it out from the millions of other sources out there. Even the computing power of our insects would take weeks to isolate the right information."

"What about their offensive capabilities?" said Queen Bee.

"The androids we've seen so far aren't armed, as such. However, there are a number of cavities built into them, at hip and chest level, which could be used to house, well –" Simon spread his arms wide – "you name it. Guns, grenades, even small rocket launchers or more specialized devices. Also, looking at their carbon-fibre frames, they're extremely strong. They could easily smash their way through a wall. Our insects are designed to withstand direct hammer blows, but one of these androids could do them severe damage!"

"Excuse me," said Nero. "Both Widow and I are

in the form of arachnids. Spiders and scorpions are not insects."

Simon smiled. "Quite right," he muttered. "We'll try to remember to call you 'bugs' instead."

"Whatever word we use," said Professor Miller, arching an eyebrow, "I have the latest system upgrades ready for installation. Chopper, you can go first."

The dragonfly detached himself from his recharger and flew across to the professor, who swung a large magnifying screen down in front of his eyes and selected a series of microscopic tools to load into the mechanical arms.

"Is this the new stealth enhancement?" said Queen Bee.

"That's right," said the professor. "On past missions, our –" he chose his words carefully – "agents … have been forced to power down in order to avoid detection. I've designed revised components, which enable them to switch into a 'stealth' operating mode. This blankets their electromagnetic activity and will prevent them from being identified by all but the most high-intensity security and surveillance equipment. Stealth mode puts a heavy drain on their internal power systems, but they'll be able to maintain it for several hours without any ill effects."

"Excellent," said Queen Bee.

"They'll be able to operate normally," continued the professor, "even when right beside one of the androids. Providing they're not seen, that is! The only problem is that we won't be able to detect them, either. We can communicate with them, but we can't track them."

Queen Bee turned to the bugs. "As soon as you can operate safely around those androids, return to the Palace of Westminster. Don't worry about clearance, I'll sort that out from here. Our three mission objectives are: firstly, find out what those androids are doing there; secondly, find out why Sir Godfrey Kite in particular has been replaced."

"Database records indicate," said Chopper, "that he is a bachelor and lives alone. Perhaps someone with no family would face less risk of detection?"

"It's possible, but I suspect there's more to it

than that."

"You think there's a link to the World Leaders' Security Conference?" said Hercules.

"It would be an enormous coincidence if there wasn't," said Queen Bee. "Sixty-seven leaders in one room. A tempting target for any criminal organization. Which brings me to our third mission objective: trace the androids back to whoever built them."

Simon Turing scrolled the 3D display. "At this point, all we can say is that manufacturing these androids must have taken time and money. There are a number of known terrorist groups who might have attempted this, but they'd all have needed very specialized scientific help."

"Tap into every database you can," said Queen Bee. "Look for anything suspicious with a link to research in robotics. Simon, you coordinate sorting through the data."

"Will do, Ms Maynard," said Simon.

"SWARM – I want you to watch, follow, gather clues and evidence," Queen Bee instructed them. "That's our best chance of tracing the villains behind this. Move in to attack only if an android is about to cause harm. If they do, take them down – fast. Questions about what's happened to the people those androids have replaced will have to wait. Our main aim must be to control the threat."

At that moment, the door of the laboratory slid back. A man and a woman, both smartly dressed, dashed in and hurried over to Queen Bee. They were known only by their code names Agent J and Agent K, and they were SWARM's human field agents.

"Bad news, Queen Bee," said Agent J, slightly out of breath.

"It's Morris Drake," said Agent K. "He's just been sprung from an MI5 safe house."

Queen Bee shut her eyes for a moment, her hands squeezing into fists. "That's all we need," she said. "When was this?"

"Less than fifteen minutes ago," Agent K said. "Initial police reports say neighbours heard explosions. The house is a wreck, two agents and a section chief are down. Drake was snatched by three people, all unidentified."

"Do you think this is linked to the android situation?" said Chopper.

"If it isn't," said Hercules, "that would be another enormous coincidence!"

Queen Bee dropped her gaze to the floor for a second, her lips pursed. Not for a moment did she allow her tough, professional exterior to show any of the nerves and uncertainty she felt inside. Life-or-death decisions rested on her leadership. She snapped to attention.

"Our mission is expanded," she said. "Nero, Hercules, Widow: go after Drake. We know he's dangerous and devious, so we can't allow him to get away. Find him by whatever means necessary. Chopper, Sirena, Morph, Sabre: proceed to the Palace of Westminster. Keep tabs on those androids and gather data. Agent K, you escort the first group. Agent J, the second group." She turned to Professor Miller. "Get those upgrades finished and launch the SWARM!"

CHAPTER FIVE

Twenty minutes later, a small two-seater sports car drew up close to the MI5 safe house where Drake had been held. SWARM's Agent K was at the wheel.

The house was cordoned off and a crime-scene-unit van was parked on the pavement outside. Officers could be seen going in and out through the wreckage of the front door.

Agent K glanced up and down the street to check that none of the police officers had noticed her arrive, then leaned across the dashboard and activated a slim panel. It slid aside with a soft hum, and a tray glided out. Embedded into dark foam padding lay Widow, Nero and Hercules. They climbed out and the tray slid back.

Agent K spoke through an encrypted channel on her smartphone. "SWARM HQ, Hive 2 are online."

"Logged, Hive 2," said Simon Turing, back at base.

"You're up, guys," said Agent K to the three robots.

Hercules held Nero tightly with his legs and took to the air. Widow spun and swung her way out of the car and up into the trees of a nearby garden. Their voices were relayed through Agent K's phone.

"We're live," reported Hercules. "We'd better work fast."

"Tapping multiple databases... Connected..." said Nero.

"Whoever has taken Drake currently has a forty-five minute lead on you," said Agent K. "The only clue we have from the police report is that a neighbour saw a dark blue car driving away from the scene. It's not exactly much to go on!

We don't even have the registration number."

By now the three robots were well out of Agent K's sight.

"Drake doesn't know about SWARM," said Nero. "We have no reason to suspect that the people in the car will know we're chasing him. They're unlikely to have changed vehicles – humans will assume that it would be impossible to be tracked down in such a big city."

"So he'll still be in that same dark blue car," said Hercules.

"Unless he's already reached wherever he's going," added Agent K.

"That's also unlikely," said Nero. "He's now a wanted fugitive. There'll be a lot of people looking for him in London. He'll be heading somewhere further away."

"Good hunting," said Agent K. She flipped her phone back into her pocket, and drove away. The police outside the damaged safe house didn't notice her go.

"Queen Bee to Hive 1."

Chopper, Sirena, Morph and Sabre had spread out to scan a number of government buildings. Sirena was back at the Palace of Westminster while Chopper and Sabre were at Downing Street and the cabinet offices in Whitehall; Morph was at the Ministry of Defence. All had switched to stealth mode.

"Hive 1 to Queen Bee," transmitted Chopper. "We're in position."

"What's the status of the Sir Godfrey android?"

"It's still in the House of Commons," said Sirena. "It seems to be doing nothing that the real Sir Godfrey wouldn't normally do. I'm making a systematic high-res scan of the entire area. Now we know what we're looking for, I can recalibrate my sensors to pick up the androids over a much greater distance. The two journalist androids are both in the public gallery overlooking the main chamber. The cleaner android is emptying bins in the offices to the west. All four are sending out scan signals. They'll find nothing now that we have the stealth upgrade. No further androids found so far."

"Good, keep me informed," said Queen Bee. "And what data have you gathered?"

"I've squeezed around a loose window frame," said Morph, "and into the casing of the laptop PC in Sir Godfrey's office. I'm about to hack into the hard drive using fibre-optic probes."

"Once you're inside the Ministry of Defence private network," said Queen Bee, "pull out every byte of data you can. There should be important clues in there somewhere."

"Logged, Queen Bee."

Nero was also soaking up data. He hacked into CCTV systems across the city and analyzed thousands of gigabytes of information, including hundreds of hours of video footage. Work that would have taken humans – or even ordinary computers – several weeks to carry out was completed in less than a minute.

"Within the correct time parameters," said Nero, "allowing a three-minute margin of error, there are five vehicles that passed the safe house and would be described by humans as 'dark blue'. No data is available from the exact street on which the safe house stands, because the CCTV recordings at the safe house were destroyed by one of the explosions. I've had to base calculations on the nearest visual sources."

"And?" said Hercules.

"All five vehicles are standard cars. One can be tracked to the car park of a supermarket. Two drove to private addresses within a mile of the safe house. One visited a coffee shop and then pulled up outside a hotel in the city centre. All of these can be eliminated from our enquiries."

"Because they've stayed within London?" said Hercules.

"Affirmative," said Nero. "And because each had only one occupant. Drake will probably be travelling with whoever freed him. The fifth car is our target. Piecing together data from three traffic cameras, this car has four people in it."

"Where's our target now?" said Hercules.

"Close to the M25," said Nero. "I haven't been able to assemble a complete record of the car's route so far, but it seems they stopped at a petrol station for seven minutes to refuel. The obvious conclusion is that they're planning quite a long journey."

"Should we signal Agent K?" said Hercules. "Could we catch up with them faster at ground level?"

"Checking current traffic conditions… Negative, a direct route at altitude will be quickest. Heavy traffic means the car is travelling slowly, and should continue to do so for approximately fourteen minutes. If you can carry me and fly at your maximum speed, and Widow matches it, we will make visual contact with the vehicle in eleven minutes, twenty seconds."

"Logged," came the reply from both Hercules and Widow.

Widow fired a micro-thin web-line at a nearby office block and zipped along it at high speed. Hercules increased power to his motor circuits, tilted his wings forward slightly and shot off in a straight line, heading north-west.

"All this data is heating up my central processors," said Morph. "Switching the laptop's internal fan on."

The centipede's gelatinous body was squashed to a thickness of only 0.9 millimetres. He was squeezed inside Sir Godfrey Kite's computer, below the hard drive and the motherboard. Tiny probes ran from between his antennae to the components around him. The computer's fan whirred into life, sending cooling air currents all around Morph.

"That's better," said Morph. "Processing Ministry of Defence records ... personal calendar and scheduling information ... personnel data... Using mainframe at SWARM HQ for additional cross-referencing..."

"What have you come up with?" asked Chopper, who was currently concealed behind a ceiling light inside Number 10 Downing Street.

"To begin with," said Morph, "there's a small discrepancy in the logs covering personnel movements last night. Sir Godfrey Kite is listed as entering this building twice yesterday, but leaving only once. Normally, we could dismiss that as simple human error, but under the circumstances, it's almost certainly significant. It may indicate that Sir Godfrey was replaced less than twelve hours before we detected his android duplicate."

"That's good news," said Chopper. "See if you can establish his movements and actions since then."

"Logged."

Suddenly, Sirena signalled from the House of Commons. "Two more androids detected!"

"Location?" said Chopper.

"They've just entered the Ministry of Defence."

"Morph, can you ID them?"

"Checking…" said Morph. "Yes, computer logs and security cameras show them both to be officials working for Sir Godfrey Kite. One of them is his personal secretary, Colin Havelock. The other is Miranda Knowles, in charge of the ministry's budget."

"Hive 1 to SWARM HQ," said Chopper.

Queen Bee was online immediately and Chopper brought her up to date.

"So now we know that six people with regular

access to government buildings have been replaced by androids," said Queen Bee. "And we don't know of any unusual or criminal actions they've carried out so far?"

"Negative," said Chopper. "Morph is analyzing the Ministry of Defence's confidential files now."

"The androids appear to be waiting," said Queen Bee thoughtfully.

"For the World Leaders' Security Conference?" said Chopper.

"Yes," said Queen Bee. "Simon and Professor Miller have been checking the robotics angle. If the people behind the androids are getting scientific help, they're not getting it from any of the world's leading researchers. The professor says there have been nine notable experts across the globe capable of producing these androids in the past five years. Right now, seven are safely accounted for, one has been unwell for many months and one died a couple of years ago. It looks like the androids' controllers are better technicians than we thought. Keep me informed. Queen Bee out."

There was a beep on the network.

"Morph," said Chopper. "Anything more yet?"

"I may not be as fast as Nero at data processing," said Morph, "but I think I've isolated exactly the information we're looking for. I've found several suspicious consignments of goods."

"What are these consignments?" said Sabre. He was currently on the underside of a table in a meeting room at the government's offices on Whitehall.

"All but one were large deliveries of electronic spare parts. They were ordered from various different suppliers by Miranda Knowles – or rather, her duplicate – over the past three weeks."

"So that particular android has been operating for nearly a month!" said Chopper.

"All the suppliers were told that the parts were for Ministry of Defence projects, and all were told to make their delivery to a remote government airfield in the north-west of England. It's located close to a woodland area in Cumbria, and is designated 11-88."

"These Ministry of Defence projects were fake?" said Chopper.

"Yes," said Morph. "After arriving at airfield

11-88, records of the deliveries vanish without trace."

"The people controlling the androids must have picked them up," said Sabre. "At least we now know why Miranda Knowles was targeted for replacement. She's in charge of the Ministry's budget and could order those spares without arousing suspicion."

"She was probably the first person to be replaced," said Chopper. "Perhaps the spare parts were used to build more androids?"

"It's the final consignment that's the most worrying one," said Morph. "It's an order for advanced weapons, due to be delivered later today. Three large crates filled with guns, grenades and explosives."

"Another faked Ministry project?" said Chopper.

"No," said Morph. "Weapons can't be ordered or moved around like other things. It's a security measure. This is a regular order, coded AE-X-4567-beta, which was supposed to go to an army base in Dorset for use in training exercises."

"It's been re-routed to 11-88?" said Chopper.

"Late last night," said Morph, "by the only person who would have the correct authority, namely the Secretary of State for Defence, Sir Godfrey Kite."

"Surely a genuine order would be missed?" said Chopper.

"Yes," said Morph, "but not until it becomes clear that nobody in the Ministry's system has actually received the weapons. By then, it will be too late. The World Leaders' Security Conference has its first session tomorrow morning at 10 a.m. According to the SWARM database, leaders are expected to begin arriving in London tonight."

"When is this re-routed delivery supposed to take place?"

"In four hours' time," said Morph. "11-88 is three hundred and ten miles away from us. What can we do?"

"Sirena," transmitted Chopper, "hold your position at the Palace of Westminster and remain on full alert."

"Logged," said Sirena.

"Sabre and Morph, we'll update Queen Bee and intercept that delivery. It's our best lead yet.

The weapons should take us directly to whoever made the androids."

"So far, none of the android replacements here have been armed," said Morph. "If they get hold of those weapons, they'll have all they need to wipe out the conference."

CHAPTER SIX

"Switching to stealth mode."

Hercules, Nero and Widow could all sense the extra power drain on their systems. They were now less than thirty metres away from the dark blue car carrying Drake and the three androids who'd freed him from the MI5 safe house. Traffic honked and shuffled below them. The micro-robots dropped down close to ground level, so that they could remain unnoticed by the drivers and passengers in the slow-moving cars.

They scuttled across the road's surface until they were beneath the car. Then they hopped up and gripped tightly on to its dirt-encrusted underside. Shortly after, the car suddenly turned left and began to accelerate.

"We're on the exhaust system muffler here," said Hercules. "I'll get us inside."

He flew up behind a tangle of pipes. The noise of the car's engine reverberated off the road, and the rear wheels spun rapidly. Once he'd located the ridged area he was looking for, Hercules swiftly cut a circular hole in the metal and climbed inside. Nero and Widow followed him, crawling along the pipes, the microscopic grippers in their legs holding firmly to the bumping, greasy surface.

On the other side of the hole, they found themselves in the car's boot. It contained only a large holdall and a jack, sitting on top of a thin piece of carpet. Ahead of them was the back of the car's rear seats.

"At this close distance," said Nero, "scans show that Drake is accompanied by three androids. One of the androids is driving, Drake is on the back seat. The car is now moving rapidly and I'm reading fewer vehicles in the immediate area. Speed is increasing. Accelerating to 61 … 63 … 65 m.p.h…"

"Satellite navigation places us on the M1, heading north towards Luton," said Hercules. "I'll transmit our status to HQ."

"I'll record everything Drake and the androids say and do," said Nero. He recalibrated his visual sensors to X-ray. "Drake is currently leaning forward past the front seats, adjusting the car radio."

Drake stabbed at the radio's pre-set buttons. Quick bursts of rock music, opera and news reports blared out, then he switched the radio off and sat back with a grunt.

"Rubbish," he muttered. He tapped the driver – the android disguised as a postman – on the shoulder.

"Where exactly are we going, then? Luton airport? Are we taking a flight?"

The android didn't answer.

"Where's Gold Leader's base?" said Drake.

"Do we have far to go?"

The android's voice was flat and emotionless. "We have a further five hundred and eighty-nine miles to travel."

"What?" spluttered Drake.

"Current estimated duration is nine hours, thirty-seven minutes," said the android.

Drake muttered something under his breath, then said, "You'll have to pull in soon. I'll need a pee."

"You should have expelled liquid waste when we stopped for fuel."

"And I'm starving!"

"You should have purchased food intake when we stopped for fuel."

"Oh, shut up!" sneered Drake. "Are all Gold Leader's androids as irritating as you lot?"

"The six androids based in London have the most advanced programming, including social-interaction modules," said the android, reciting lines from its memory store. "We are functional to Level 7B, while worker androids at Silverclaw base are—"

"Yeah, yeah, button it," moaned Drake. "It was

a rhetorical question." He slumped back in his seat and stared out of the window.

In the car's boot, the micro-robots immediately began transmitting this new information to SWARM HQ.

"Checking databases..." said Nero. "No references to a 'Silverclaw' at MI5 or MI6. Widening search criteria..."

"Let's see now," said Hercules. "A journey of five hundred and eighty-nine miles will place us ... somewhere in the Scottish Highlands."

"Come in, SWARM HQ. Approaching drop zone."

"Logged." Simon Turing's voice sounded tinny inside Agent K's flight helmet. She dipped the nose of the military stealth jet fighter and the gently curving horizon slid into view in front of her. The sun had just set, and the sky was streaked with orange and red, but Agent K's goggles showed the landscape below her as a detailed green glow surrounded by readouts on the aircraft's altitude and course.

"Reducing speed," said Agent K. "Falling to 10,000 metres, ready for payload drop." She banked the fighter to the right, then levelled off. "Airfield 11-88 dead ahead, HQ."

"SWARM ready?" asked Simon.

"Affirmative," signalled Chopper.

Chopper, Morph and Sabre were packed into a thick liquid within a transparent plastic sphere about the size of a tennis ball. The sphere was loaded into a specially modified rocket launcher fitted beneath the fighter's wing.

"Coming up on drop zone," said Agent K. "Five seconds … four … three … two … releasing now!"

She flicked a switch on the control board in front of her. The rocket launcher shot the plastic sphere into the air with a loud popping sound.

The fighter veered off to the right and flew back the way it had come, the roar of its jet engine gradually fading to a low boom. Meanwhile, the sphere tumbled down, buffeted by the wind, until it finally hit grass. It bounced twice and rolled to a stop.

The sphere beeped and split in half, and the

three micro-robots crawled out, shaking the liquid off them. Both the sphere and the liquid were designed to biodegrade within an hour of landing, leaving no trace. The robots scuttled across the grass to get their bearings.

"Agent K is a good shot," said Sabre. "We're right in the middle of airfield 11-88. The delivery of weapons is scheduled to be in sixteen minutes."

"This place looks abandoned," said Morph.

The airfield was little more than a large flat expanse of grass surrounded by a high chain-link fence. At the far end of the field were a couple of small shed-like buildings and, attached to the fence beside an entrance gate was a metal sign saying "Ministry of Defence – KEEP OUT".

Beyond the airfield was plain, featureless moorland stretching for miles and dense woodland to the east. It was growing dark, and the wind was picking up.

"Visual circuits to night vision," said Chopper. "Airfield 11-88 was set up during World War II. It's hardly been used since. The Ministry keep it for emergency use, or for top-secret training exercises."

"It's certainly a lonely spot," said Morph.

At that moment, all three robots picked up the sound of an approaching helicopter. It was still several miles away, beyond human earshot.

"Bearing 382.2," said Chopper, "coming in at low altitude. Are we all clear on the agreed plan?"

"Affirmative," replied Morph and Sabre.

Before the robots had left SWARM HQ, Queen Bee and Professor Miller had told the robots to stay close to the weapons. Thanks to Drake, they now knew that the delivery would be taken to "Silverclaw". The robots were not to attempt to intercept the weapons.

But Simon Turing and Alfred Berners had argued that allowing Silverclaw to receive the weapons could pose too great a risk.

Chopper had come up with a clever solution to both problems – and one that meant Silverclaw would never know what had happened.

The sharp beam of a helicopter searchlight appeared in the distance. It swept along the ground ahead as it rapidly approached the airfield.

The robots switched to stealth mode.

Within seconds, the helicopter touched down

on to the grass, about twenty metres from the robots, its rotors whipping up a storm. It had a cargo hold at the rear, and was painted in dark camouflage colours. The whine of its engines slowly died away.

Two figures got out of the cockpit, both wearing British army uniforms. One was dressed as a colonel.

"Androids," confirmed Chopper.

The robots quickly moved towards them, keeping hidden from sight. They took up position beside the helicopter and waited, still and silent. A few minutes later, the rumble of a small lorry cut across the low moan of the wind. Headlights bumped into view as the lorry swayed along a muddy track to the gate. Someone got out of the cab, opened the gate and waved the lorry through.

It was a standard green army vehicle and SWARM analysis confirmed the four soldiers were human. A captain in a peaked cap walked over to the androids carrying a torch, while three officer cadets piled out of the lorry and unhooked the drop-down section at the back. Inside were three large crates.

The captain saluted when he saw the colonel. "Evening, sir," he nodded. "Do you have the Transfer Order ready for me to sign?"

The androids didn't answer for a moment.

"There is no order," said the colonel android. "This is a top-secret security matter."

"No Transfer Order, sir?" said the captain. "I, umm … wasn't informed."

"Sir!" called one of the soldiers from the back of the lorry. "Are we loading these crates?"

"Oh, er… Yes, carry on!" called the captain.

The men began hauling the heavy wooden crates off the lorry and carrying the first towards the helicopter.

On Chopper's signal, he and Sabre flew up into the helicopter's cargo compartment. Chopper carried Morph with him. They kept to the shadows, moving only when no human or android was looking in their direction.

The captain cleared his throat. "Sorry, sir, but you know what the procurement pen-pushers are like for paperwork. They'll have me on a charge if they don't get their signed Transfer Order.

What am I supposed to tell them?"

The android gazed at him. "This is a top-secret security matter," said the colonel.

The officer frowned. He stared back at the two androids for a moment. "What sort of security matter? I'm sorry, sir, but I haven't been told about any of this."

"It's top secret."

"What base did you fly out from?"

"This is a security matter. Are you questioning my authority?"

"No, sir, of course not!" said the captain. "But … who's your C.O.?"

"You are not allowed to question us."

The captain swung his torch so it shone into the androids' faces. Like the androids who had freed Drake, they looked completely human, but neither of them flinched or shielded their eyes from the glare of the beam.

The captain was clearly getting nervous. "Right, both of you. Names, rank, serial number, you know the drill. There's something fishy going on here. Osgood!"

"Sir?" answered one of the squaddies.

"How many crates have you loaded on to the helicopter?" said the captain, keeping his eyes firmly on the androids.

"Two, sir."

"Well, take them both off again."

"Sir?"

"You heard what I said, jump to it!"

Inside the helicopter's cargo compartment, the SWARM robots watched as the grumbling squaddies heaved one of the crates back out.

The two androids began to walk towards the captain.

"We require the weapons," said the colonel android.

"They're needed for a top-secret security matter," said the second android.

The captain took several steps back. He drew his pistol.

"Stay right where you are!" he cried.

The androids continued to advance. Alarmed, the three soldiers stopped what they were doing.

The captain raised his pistol. "I warn you! Halt! That is a direct order!"

The androids continued to advance.

The pistol gave two sharp cracks. The captain had fired at their legs, to wound them. Despite the smoking bullet holes just above their knees, the androids didn't even pause.

The captain fired again, this time at their chests. The androids continued to advance.

"Draw arms!" cried the captain, his voice suddenly cracking with fear. "Fire at will!"

The three squaddies dropped the heavy crate they were carrying on to the grass and reached for their guns.

"Those androids could kill them!" said Sabre. He darted out into the darkness, microscopic pellets loaded into his needle-like mouthparts.

The captain and his men fired shot after shot. A bullet glanced off the head of one of the androids. Its face tore, but it didn't slow down. Both androids raised their arms, clearly intending to either throttle their opponents or hurl them aside.

Suddenly the captain yelped and collapsed to the ground. For a second, the three squaddies gazed at him in horror, then one by one they fell. As the last one cried out and keeled over, the androids dropped their arms to their sides.

"Tranquilizer stings delivered," reported Sabre. The tiny mosquito remained close to the ground, circling around the helicopter so that he could return to the cargo compartment without risking detection. The androids, meanwhile, turned to look at each other.

"I think they may be wondering what just happened," said Chopper.

"Let's hope their programming is basic enough to let them simply accept it and carry on," said Morph.

The androids remained motionless for a moment, then they split up. The first one walked over to the lorry and picked up the third of the wooden crates. The second android picked up the crate that the squaddies had just removed from the helicopter. Both of them carried the heavy loads as if they weighed no more than a box of breakfast cereal.

While the androids slid the crates into the cargo hold, Sabre darted back inside and the SWARM robots remained there, their stealth-mode upgrades keeping them safe from scan detection. Chopper transmitted an update to SWARM HQ and requested assistance for the soldiers.

"They're unharmed," said Sabre. "They'll sleep for around twelve hours, and will remember nothing about what's happened here."

The androids climbed back into the cockpit. The helicopter's rotors began to turn, faster and faster. Moments later it rose into the night sky and flew off at speed, heading north.

"Stage one complete," said Chopper. "We're following the movement of the crates. Now to begin stage two."

CHAPTER SEVEN

Roughly two hundred and seventy miles north of airfield 11-88, the dark blue car carrying Drake finally arrived at its destination: a tiny cottage on the windswept west coast of Scotland.

The car had rumbled along a stony path for almost a mile after leaving the main road, its headlights casting sharp pools of light. When it came to a stop, and the engine was switched off, the sudden silence woke Drake up. He grunted and blinked.

"At last," he grumbled.

In the boot, Nero, Hercules and Widow

quickly crawled back through the hole Hercules had made and dropped down on to the gravel beneath the car. They left just in time to avoid being seen by one of the androids, as he opened the boot to remove the holdall.

Drake looked around, flexing his legs. A full moon bathed the landscape in a cool, eerie glow. In front of the little cottage he could make out open countryside. From behind it came the steady rhythm of the sea washing up against the coastline. The rolling waters glittered in the moonlight and about two hundred metres offshore, the long, craggy hump of an island was just visible.

"Where the devil are we?" asked Drake.

The three androids said nothing. They led him over to the cottage and the SWARM robots followed. Hercules flew close to Drake's feet and fired a tiny tracker egg at the bottom hem of his right trouser leg. The tracker attached, allowing the robots and SWARM HQ to keep tabs on Drake at all times.

"Just in case," said Hercules.

"It seems there's an error in our mapping

database," said Nero. "GPS places us at a point on the west coast of Scotland looking out towards North Uist and the Isle of Harris. That small island out there isn't included in the data."

"Perhaps it only appears at low tide," suggested Hercules, "and it's underwater most of the time."

One of the androids knocked loudly on the door of the cottage. It was answered by an old man wearing a tattered cardigan and a pair of slippers.

"Ah, nice to see you all," he said.

"Mercury 6, Mercury 9 and Mercury 10 reporting," said the android. He handed the old man the holdall.

"Come in, Mr Drake, come in," smiled the old man. "I'm afraid my home is rather basic, but at least it's comfortable."

Cautiously, Drake stepped inside.

The old man spoke to the androids. "Off you trot, you three. Let Gold Leader know Mr Drake is safe and sound." Without a word, they turned and walked back to the car.

The SWARM robots quickly scuttled inside the cottage before the door closed. They hid beneath a dusty old wooden cabinet that stood in the hallway.

"Where is Gold Leader?" demanded Drake. "I thought I was being taken to Silverclaw!"

"All in good time, Mr Drake," smiled the old man. "No need for fuss. You're to wait here until Gold Leader sends for you. Those are my orders."

"Right," said Drake. "I need a toilet and some food!"

"Of course. The bathroom is at the end of the corridor, there," the old man said.

Drake pushed past him and hurried along the hall. "I'll do you some bacon and eggs, with a nice cup of tea." The old man held up the holdall. "You've got clean clothes, too."

"Oh," said Hercules. "It looks like that tracker egg won't be any use after all."

In the control room of the Silverclaw base, Gold Leader watched the seconds tick away on one of the display screens beside her chair. Her electronic eye gleamed brighter than her real one, and her thin lips curled into a grin.

"The first delegates will be arriving in London about now," she muttered. "Presidents, prime ministers, party chairmen." She glanced around at the faceless worker androids manning the control panels. "Not long now."

She tapped a code into a communicator at her side. A nearby screen flicked into life, showing the cockpit of the helicopter transporting the stolen weapons.

"Silverclaw to Mercury 5, this is Gold Leader. What is your status?" she said.

"Acknowledged, Gold Leader, this is Mercury 5," said the android piloting the helicopter. "Weapons shipment has been acquired. We are on our way back to base. As ordered, we are flying at low altitude to avoid radar detection, and away from densely populated areas."

"Wait a minute," said Gold Leader, leaning forward in her chair. "What's happened to Mercury 2? What happened to its face?"

"The unit sustained damage," replied the android.

"How?"

"Bullets were fired at us by the army personnel delivering the consignment."

Gold Leader froze in alarm. "Why?"

"Unknown. They were suspicious of us," said the android.

"Why?" spat Gold Leader. "What happened? You were supposed to just get the crates and leave! It was a simple pick-up job!"

"One of them began asking unforeseen questions."

"For what reason?"

"Unknown," said the android.

Gold Leader thought for a moment. The fingers of her mechanical arm tapped impatiently at the side of the screen. "And were these army personnel dealt with?"

"Yes, they were dealt with," replied the android.

"Good. Get back here as soon as you can. Gold Leader out!"

She switched off the communicator with an angry stab, then got up and walked over to one of the nearby androids. The artificial limbs on her right side whirred as she moved.

"First those odd scans," she said. "Now the

army get suspicious for no apparent reason. There's something going on. I'll bet Drake's at the bottom of this – I never trusted him. Get him in here! Now!"

"Acknowledged," said the android.

"Acknowledged," said the old man. He was speaking into an antique landline phone, which was perched on top of the cabinet in the hallway.

Beneath the cabinet, the three SWARM robots monitored everything. They had been busy scanning the cottage's interior.

"I'd need to access the landline cable to tap into the conversation," said Nero, "but we can easily guess what's being said at the other end."

"Yes, yes, I'll send him along straight away," said the old man. "Goodbye." He carefully replaced the receiver.

"Do you think Drake knows that the old man is an android, too?" said Hercules.

"Probably not," said Nero. "The old man is a more-advanced model than the three who brought him here in the car. It's identical to the ones back at the Palace of Westminster."

"And do you think Drake realizes there's a transport pod built into the cupboard under the stairs?" Hercules added.

"Definitely not," said Nero. "This cottage is designed to look old-fashioned and dusty, and the old man is meant to stop humans from examining it too closely. The android is a form of guard dog."

"My X-ray probes are showing that Drake is changing clothes," said Hercules. "The tracker egg I placed will be left behind. If we're going to stay with him, perhaps we should hide ourselves in that travel pod."

"Logged," said Nero and Widow.

The three micro-robots scuttled towards the cupboard under the stairs. The old man was shuffling away along the hall. He stopped at a door and knocked gingerly.

"Mr Drake? Are you decent?" Drake emerged wearing a fresh shirt, jacket and trousers. "I hope you liked your bacon and eggs?"

"I've had better," grunted Drake. "Who was that on the phone?"

"The time has arrived! I've been asked to send you on your way to Silverclaw central control."

"Right, where are we going?" said Drake, marching towards the front door.

"Oh, no, no, Mr Drake," smiled the old man. "In here." He opened the understairs cupboard, and pulled out a vacuum cleaner. "I'll just get this out of your way."

Drake stared at him, his mouth pulled into a sneer. "What are you talking about? Are you expecting me to crawl into a cupboard?"

"Oh, it's quite roomy, really," said the old man. He motioned for Drake to step inside.

Reluctantly Drake bent over and walked into the cupboard. There was a small, battered seat fixed to the rear wall, which looked like it had been salvaged from an old car. The micro-robots were safely hidden under the car seat's springy base. Widow quickly spun a series of strong web-lines around the three of them, to keep them strapped in place. Drake sat, eyeing his surroundings warily. The inside of the cupboard seemed every bit as tattered and grubby as the rest of the place.

"You'll need to fasten your safety belt, Mr Drake," said the old man.

Drake did so slowly, his expression growing more uncertain every second.

"Scans of the earth immediately below us indicate a sudden vertical drop, then a sharp turn to the right," said Nero.

The old man gently closed the door, then flicked a light switch nearby. Inside the cupboard, there was a sudden clang as metal clamps opened. The seat and a small section of the surrounding floor instantly fell five metres down a narrow tunnel lined with metal, running on rails like a rollercoaster.

Drake screamed in terror as the travel pod swung violently to the right and shot forward.

"A very interesting piece of engineering," said Nero calmly.

At that moment, the helicopter carrying the stolen weapons was approaching the remote stretch of Scottish coastline where the cottage stood.

"I'm picking up one of Hercules's tracker eggs," said Morph.

"Confirmed," said Sabre. "Calculating location... It's in a small cottage, a few hundred metres ahead of us. No significant sound or movement close by."

"He must have tagged Drake," said Morph. "Could that little cottage really be Silverclaw's headquarters?"

"Nero, Hercules and Widow are in the area, but their signals are blurred," said Sabre. "That may be a side effect of stealth mode, or they may be deep underground. The signals are moving at high speed."

"Hive 1 to Hive 2," transmitted Chopper.

"Hive 2 online," signalled Nero from the tunnel. He sent Chopper an update on the events of the past few hours.

"What's that screaming noise?" said Chopper.

"It's Drake," said Nero. "Some humans seem to fear rapid motion."

"Your transmissions are unclear. Contact us when you can re-establish a secure link."

"Logged," said Nero. "Hive 2 out."

The helicopter began to descend.

"We should leave the helicopter before it lands," said Chopper. "We can make a full search of the area, and then find a way into Silverclaw's HQ."

"Logged," replied Sabre.

They scuttled down to a hatch at the base of the cargo hold, which led to the landing gear. Morph squeezed into the tiny gap at the edge of the hatch. He expanded and twisted his gelatinous exoskeleton, forcing the hatch to pop open, which allowed the robots to crawl through.

Moments later, they dropped out beneath the helicopter. Chopper carried Morph on his back. The centipede had to hold on tightly, as the fierce downdraft from the aircraft buffeted the tiny robots violently.

As the helicopter moved ahead of them, Hercules and Chopper managed to steady their flight.

Chopper suddenly noticed the island Nero had pointed out earlier. "I've detected something strange," he said. "Visual and satellite data places us at a known point on the Scottish coast. However, that small island positioned two hundred and four metres off the shore doesn't appear on any database I can access."

Sabre ran some checks of his own. "Confirmed," he said.

"Look!" said Morph. "The helicopter is heading straight for it. It isn't landing at the cottage at all."

The aircraft had slowed and was turning in mid-air. It descended gradually and made a perfect landing on a flattened patch of earth towards one side of the island.

"Silverclaw might be using the island to store equipment," said Morph.

The robots flew closer. As the helicopter's rotors wound down, the two androids began to unload the crates. Chopper zoomed in and observed the crates being lowered through an opening in the ground.

"I'm trying to direct probes at it, to see how much equipment might be there," said Sabre, "but all I'm reading is earth and vegetation. There must be some sort of chamber below, but nothing registers."

"There are high concentrations of metallic elements in the soil," said Chopper. "They help mask long-range sensors. We need to get closer."

The robots flew low across the choppy waters, waves rolling around them. As they approached the island, they saw the two androids follow the crates down into the opening.

The SWARM agents landed on a rocky area a few metres in front of the helicopter.

"I don't think this is simply a storage facility," said Sabre. "I'm reading multiple rooms, advanced electronics and several power sources."

"There's a small fusion reactor down there," said Chopper, "linked to a series of machines. This must be Silverclaw's headquarters."

"That's not all," said Sabre. "The island is a vehicle. It can move!"

CHAPTER EIGHT

At that exact moment, Nero the scorpion was coming to the same conclusion. "There's only one logical explanation – this base is mobile."

The tunnel from the cottage had led under the shoreline and out to the island. As soon as the travel pod came to a halt, and a bulkhead sealed behind it, Drake had got to his feet and stalked off.

Nero, Hercules and Widow were now concealed in the shadows on top of a tall bank of switches in the main control room of Silverclaw's HQ. Below them, androids moved around the room from screen to screen, monitoring and making adjustments. A low hum of energy throbbed throughout the base.

On the other side of the control room, Gold Leader and Morris Drake were arguing.

"I took a considerable risk getting you away from MI5," said Gold Leader. "Be grateful."

"Oh, I am, I am," said Drake, raising his hands. "But it's not like you to take risks. I thought my part in your scheme had ended. I'm flattered that I'm so important to our masters."

Gold Leader suddenly lunged at him and grasped his collar with her mechanical hand. "I didn't do it for them," she spat. "I did it for me! They might be content to leave you in the hands of the enemy, but I'm not. I've brought you here because odd things have been happening. I want answers! I won't have this operation sabotaged by the likes of you."

Drake angrily pulled himself free. "The likes of me? That's rich, coming from a half-robot!"

Gold Leader's face flushed with fury. For several seconds, she fought to control her temper. When she finally spoke, her voice was low and venomous. "In London, my most important unit, the replacement Sir Godfrey Kite, was the subject of a scan of unknown origin."

"What sort of scan?"

"If I knew that, you idiot, it's origin wouldn't be unknown, would it?" shouted Gold Leader. "It was sophisticated, and it was right inside the House of Commons. You didn't warn me about such systems!"

"I didn't know they existed," said Drake.

"While you were a member of MI5," snarled Gold Leader, "you had access to everything on UK government security. You were supposed to supply me with details of every system installed in every building in Westminster."

"And I did!"

"Oh, but this one thing you just happened to overlook, is that it?"

"Tomorrow," sneered Drake, "you are going to blow up sixty-seven heads of state! Do you really think they're not going to boost security in the days before a World Leaders' Security Conference?"

"You should have informed me!" cried Gold Leader. "All systems, all possibilities!"

"There are undercover sections of the secret service that even I don't have access to! There's one in the Secret Intelligence Agency that ruined two of my own operations, and I don't even know what it's called!"

In the shadows, Hercules flexed his wings. "Well, well, I think he's talking about us."

"We should inform SWARM HQ at once that Silverclaw intends to detonate a bomb at the World Leaders' Security Conference," said Nero. "Wait a minute… My network signals can't get through the barrier that's on top of this island."

"Testing…" said Hercules. "Mine neither."

"We could increase power," suggested Widow.

"We can't do that," said Nero, "without reducing the stealth effect and exposing us to discovery. For the moment, we will have to stay out of contact."

"Hive 1 to Hive 2." Chopper's voice suddenly cut into the robots' communications network. "We have entered the base, through an engine vent located beneath the waterline."

"Perfect timing," said Hercules.

"Hive 2 to Hive 1," said Nero. "Outside contact

functions are restricted in here. One of you should go back outside and update HQ. Silverclaw are planning to detonate a bomb at the conference tomorrow."

"Logged," said Sabre. "I'll go."

While Sabre buzzed back towards the vent, Chopper and Morph began to make their way through the base towards Nero, Hercules and Widow. In the control room, Gold Leader gave orders to the two androids who'd flown in the helicopter.

"Mercury 5, load the weapons for the main strike into our armoury here. Were the contents of the crates as expected?"

"Yes," said Mercury 5.

"Then use the high explosives to make up the bomb for tomorrow, and get that back on to the helicopter. Take enough arms for the Platinum units, too. Then get to London as fast as possible."

"Acknowledged," said Mercury 5.

She turned to the other android. "Mercury 2, when you get to London, make sure the van is in place at the correct time. And repair that damaged face of yours before you go."

"Acknowledged," said Mercury 2. Both of them left the control room.

"So Gold Leader is a mixture of human and machine," said Hercules.

"The correct word is 'cyborg'," said Nero.

"I wonder how she ended up like that," said Hercules.

"Cross-checking internal mission databanks…" said Nero. "Her facial features match those of a woman named Alexis Vendetti, who was reported killed in an accident one year, eleven months and four days ago. She is one of the experts in robotics that HQ were checking up on earlier. Since she is listed as dead, they would have made no further enquiries."

"How could she have vanished?" said Widow.

"She was known as someone who held extremist political views," said Nero. "She supported a number of brutal dictatorships in Eastern Europe and Africa. Alexis Vendetti was directing the construction of an automated factory in the Far East when a power unit exploded. Ninety people died and it was assumed that she had been buried under tonnes of rubble.

The government she was working for wanted to cover up the incident, and have never officially admitted it took place at all. They simply bulldozed the site. Her body was never found."

"I can understand why she's angry," said Hercules.

Gold Leader was pacing the floor of the control room, her artificial limbs whirring. "I don't trust you, Drake."

"The feeling's mutual, I assure you," sneered Drake.

"If you've withheld information from me, what have you not told our masters?"

"I've withheld nothing!" shouted Drake. "How dare you imply that—"

"MI5 had you captive for weeks! What did you tell them? Did you offer them a deal? Did you promise to spill your guts about Silverclaw in return for your freedom?"

"Of course not! They threatened me, they offered me bribes, but they never got a word out of me! Not a single word!"

Nero checked the data. "Analysis of Drake's body language and heart rate shows he's lying."

"With Drake, that's hardly a surprise," said Hercules.

Gold Leader stared directly into Drake's deep-set eyes. "Why do I have difficulty believing a slimy little worm who'd switch sides and betray his country, just for money?"

"An awful lot of money," smiled Drake. "MI5 pay isn't all it should be, you know. Don't worry, I'm loyal. As long as the price is right. Perhaps it's your loyalty we should question? Why are you supporting our masters' goal of world domination? You're their puppet, just as I am. How do we know you're not going to turn your androids against them? Perhaps someone who's mostly mechanical is more likely to side with the machines?"

With a yell of rage, Gold Leader landed a punch on Drake's jaw. He spun on his heels and collapsed to the floor. He scrambled to sit up, dabbing the back of his hand to the fresh cut on his lip.

"Yes, that's a touchy subject with you, isn't it?" he grinned. "Being less than a real person."

"Agents for our masters saved my life!" growled Gold Leader. "They dragged me from the wreckage, near to death. They financed this operation and let me run it. They valued me and my skills in robotics when I was abandoned by the rest of the world. Now the rest of the world will pay! And you, a miserable turncoat, question my loyalty?"

Gold Leader's mechanical arm grasped Drake's throat. She lifted him up and off his feet. He struggled for breath.

"I'll give you one last chance," she hissed. "Tell me everything you know!"

"There's nothing more I can tell you!" croaked Drake, his face going red. "Everything I know, you know!"

Gold Leader tightened her grip on him. She held his face close to hers. "Tomorrow, the World Leaders' Security Conference will be destroyed. There will be chaos. And while there are accusations and wars, and confusion on a global scale, our masters will step in and take over half the countries of the world. Our revolution will have begun. And you know what? I'm going to make sure that they realize what snivelling pond scum you really are. Your life won't be worth living."

She flung Drake aside. A pair of androids caught him, holding him upright as he coughed and spluttered.

"Take him away!" spat Gold Leader. "I'll hand him over after the main strike. In the meantime, I want him safely out of the picture. Put him on ice!"

"Acknowledged," replied the androids. They marched Drake out of the control room.

"Hive 2 to Hive 1," transmitted Nero.

"I wonder who these mysterious masters of theirs are," said Hercules.

"Hive 1 online," answered Chopper, in response to Nero's signal.

"Drake is being taken towards your position. Can you monitor him?"

"We're picking him up now," said Chopper. The programs in his visual circuits cycled through X-ray, motion detection and bio-scan modes, getting a detailed picture of Drake.

The androids hauled Drake along, down a

corridor and past a sliding door marked "Cryonic Storage". Drake struggled and protested all the way.

Chopper, carrying Morph in his legs, whipped through the gap just as the door slid shut.

Inside, arranged along the length of one wall, were a series of tall transparent tubes. Six of them were occupied by the six humans who'd been replaced by androids back in London. They stood motionless, surrounded by a green mist, their eyes closed.

"We've discovered the whereabouts of the real Sir Godfrey Kite and the others," signalled Chopper. "They're held in suspended animation."

"Why has Gold Leader kept them alive?" mused Morph. "Wouldn't it make more sense to dispose of them?"

"Logically," signalled Nero from the control room, "they are being kept alive in case specific knowledge they have is needed by their android replacements. Obscure pass codes, for example, or information about other people. It's also possible that they might be returned to their normal places after tomorrow's 'main strike', making it appear that they were responsible for the destruction."

One of the androids tapped a seven-digit code into a keypad beside an empty tube. It rotated to reveal an open section, just the right size for a human.

"No, no, no!" cried Drake. "I'm not getting in there! No way!"

Without a word, the androids bundled him inside and tapped a second code into the keypad. The tube rotated, and Drake was engulfed in green mist. Gradually, his eyelids drooped and closed.

"This is a very worrying development," said Morph. "Now that we've pinpointed the location of this base, SWARM HQ may send an attack force to destroy it before Gold Leader can disappear by moving the base out to sea, or along the coast. The lives of these humans may be in great danger."

"Sabre," signalled Chopper, "have you left the base? Have you made that transmission to HQ yet?"

"Negative," reported Sabre. "The vent we entered through has been automatically sealed.

Not even Morph could squeeze through. We must have come in while the engine was routinely venting heat. I've been trying to find another way out, without success."

"Unless we can warn HQ that there are innocent humans here," said Morph, "they could be killed."

"SWARM HQ may not realize we've located the base," said Chopper. "We've been in stealth mode for some time, which means they can't detect us any more than the androids can."

"Just so long as they don't launch an attack," said Morph.

"You're forgetting one thing," said Hercules. "Something left back at the cottage."

"The tracker egg will allow us to pinpoint our attack," said Simon Turing.

Back in the laboratory at SWARM HQ in London, Simon was operating a large display screen for Queen Bee, Professor Miller and Alfred Berners to observe. The screen showed tactical data overlaid on a map of the Scottish coastline.

"Are we sure that the tracker egg is at Silverclaw's base?" said Alfred.

"Not one hundred per cent," admitted Simon, "but it's barely moved since it was placed. It could be attached to Drake, who could simply be fast asleep, after all it's –" he checked his smartwatch – "past one in the morning now. We know Drake's destination was Silverclaw's headquarters, from what was said on the car journey."

"What's the latest from the bugs?" said Queen Bee.

"They were reporting in regularly," said Simon, "but we've heard nothing for a while now. They may be experiencing transmission difficulties, if they're having to maintain stealth mode at full power."

"Hmm," mused Queen Bee. "That upgrade needs further work. Professor, we need to examine our programme of enhancements for the robots. It's vital that SWARM stays one step ahead of our enemies in terms of technology."

"Refinements to stealth mode and other systems are already in hand, Ms Maynard," said the professor.

"What about the conference?" said Alfred Berners. "Any luck?"

Queen Bee let out a long breath. "I spoke to the prime minister less than an hour ago. There is no way he'll allow the conference to move venue or be cancelled. He says it would set alarm bells ringing among the delegates, and jeopardize the delicate negotiations that will be taking place. His exact words were 'ensuring security and preventing attacks is what the secret service is for, now go and do your job'. He was not in the best of moods."

"Oh dear," said Simon, pulling a face.

"I take it you couldn't tell him the full story?" said Alfred. "Reveal the existence of SWARM and what we're really facing, I mean?"

"No," said Queen Bee. "As always, we can only operate on a need-to-know basis. MI5's checks on him show he might talk under pressure. That door is firmly closed. Meanwhile, Simon, what are local conditions at the site?"

Simon flipped the display over to a detailed night-vision view of the area surrounding the cottage and Silverclaw's base. "There's a full moon and a clear sky, with no change predicted in the forecast. Visibility should be excellent, although naturally that means it'll be excellent for the enemy, too."

"And the base itself?" said Queen Bee.

"The only structure is this small cottage," said Simon, circling a shape on the map with his finger. "I started with the assumption that the base itself is located underground, with this cottage as a disguised entry point. However, I spotted an oddity."

He reached up and circled another shape.

"What's that?" said Queen Bee. "A boat moored offshore?"

"That would seem to be the most sensible answer," said Simon. "The trouble is, satellite imagery shows it to be an island. There are loads of little islands off that stretch of coast. Nothing peculiar there. Except that this one doesn't appear on any maps. It's popped up out of nowhere."

Alfred peered at the screen over the top of his spectacles. "If it's a boat or a submarine, it's a large one."

"I'm certain that is Silverclaw's headquarters," said Simon. "Some sort of camouflaged vehicle under the water."

"I think you're right," said Queen Bee. "I'll update Agent K. She'll be leading the attack on the base, assisted by a squadron of MI5 agents. They think she's an officer with MI6. They're a short distance from the target area, waiting for the go ahead."

"And the androids in London?" said Alfred.

"Agent J will be in charge of a large group of heavily armed police, stationed in and around Westminster. They will round up the six androids. The police think Agent J is a senior detective from Scotland Yard."

Queen Bee paused for a moment. "These operations," she said at last, "must take place at exactly the same time. The attack on Silverclaw's headquarters and the capture of the androids must be coordinated precisely. If one takes place before the other, we may lose everything. If the androids discover that the base has been destroyed, we don't know what their programming will tell them to do. If the base hears that the androids have been put out of action, they could easily have a back-up plan in place that we cannot even guess at. Only a carefully timed effort can succeed. Silverclaw must be eliminated in one decisive hit."

"Understood," said Simon Turing.

"What will decide the timing?" said Alfred Berners.

"Sirena," said Queen Bee. "She's been keeping a constant monitor on the six android replacements in Westminster. As soon as we get the slightest indication that Silverclaw are preparing to strike, as soon as one of those androids makes any kind of suspicious move, that's when we go. Simon, can you check on her status, please?"

Simon tapped a series of keys on the display screen. It switched to a mid-air, night-vision view of a smart Georgian building. Readouts along the bottom of the display showed Sirena's exact position as a few streets away from the Palace of Westminster.

"SWARM HQ to Sirena," said Simon. "Report."

"Sirena to SWARM HQ," Sirena's electronic

voice came out over the speakers. "The androids have continued to act exactly like the people they've replaced. No changes from expected routines, journeys or activities. Silverclaw chose their victims well. None have families or close friends who might have become suspicious. Their programming has made sure they behave normally at all times. However, there has been a development."

"What's that building up ahead?" said Simon.

"The block of flats where Sir Godfrey Kite lives," said Sirena. "I've tracked all six androids to this location. This is the first unusual activity they've shown. I think something may be about to happen."

The humans in the laboratory exchanged glances, their eyes wide.

"Right," said Simon. "There's no way those six people would assemble at Sir Godfrey's home. Certainly not in the middle of the night."

"I'm reading all of them inside the flat now," said Sirena. "I'll be inside their detection range in a matter of seconds. I'll switch to stealth mode."

The screen suddenly filled with static then Sirena's voice returned.

"Ten metres from the living-room window," she transmitted. "My sensors are picking up movement. Wait, they've stopped… Stand by…"

The seconds ticked away.

"What's your status, Sirena?" said Queen Bee.

"I'm inside the living room, beside a chair. The androids are sitting motionless. Their internal electronics are still active, but their more complex functions appear to be on standby. They seem to be waiting for something. I'll fly closer. If I can land on one of them, I might be able to intercept its deep-core programming and hack its databank."

"Be careful," said Queen Bee.

"Logged, Queen Bee," said Sirena. "I have stealth mode at full power, so they won't detect a probe signal."

"Moving in closer to the Sir Godfrey Kite android…" transmitted Sirena. "All six of them are simply sitting here… I'm going to try to—"

Suddenly, her voice was cut off. A high-pitched tone came from the speaker, making the humans jump.

"Sirena?" said Queen Bee. "Sirena? Report!" Silence. "Sirena!"

"Platinum 1 to Silverclaw." The voice, identical to that of Sir Godfrey Kite, issued from the communications unit attached to Gold Leader's chair.

"What is it?" snapped Gold Leader. "You're supposed to be waiting for my signal to begin the main strike!"

"Something you should see," replied Platinum 1. He swung the smartphone he was using, so that its camera pointed to something crumpled up in the palm of his hand.

Gold Leader peered at the screen in front of her. "You crushed a butterfly?" she said, her voice trembling with anger. "You called me to say you've crushed a butterfly?"

The SWARM micro-robots had spread out across the control room, looking for a way into the base's electronic systems. They paused when they heard Gold Leader's words.

"Sirena!" said Morph.

"Platinum 1 to Platinum 6 are at Sir Godfrey's

flat, as ordered," said Platinum 1. "My visual processors picked up a small insect. Platinum-level programming enables investigation of minor anomalies, therefore I snatched it up. It's mechanical."

"What?" roared Gold Leader. "What is it, a surveillance device? A camera? Is it still operating?"

"No, the pressure of my fist has deactivated it."

"MI5!" spat Gold Leader. "Their mobile CCTV must be more advanced than I've been told. They know about us! I won't allow the Silverclaw operation to fail!"

Gold Leader swiped the screen and called up a virtual keyboard. Out of her mechanical hand whirred an electronic security key. It was a narrow, cylindrical probe, covered in complex circuitry, which she slotted into a port beside the screen and twisted. It beeped. Her other hand tapped out several lines of computer code. Platinum 1's phone decoded it and displayed a square QR barcode which Platinum 1's eyes read as a simple message: "Emergency order 4-alpha-7 –

switch to plan two."

"Acknowledged," said Platinum 1. He encoded a reply to Gold Leader: "4-alpha-7 begins – replace faces, change clothes, move to separate locations, bomb and weapons to be collected according to revised Plan 2 schedule."

"What are they saying?" said Hercules.

"We need to hack into their systems as fast as possible," said Chopper. "Hercules, start cutting holes in the back of those control consoles."

"Get out of that flat and prepare for the main strike," said Gold Leader.

"Acknowledged. Platinum 1 out."

Gold Leader spun around and barked orders at the nearest android. "If they know about the London cell, they might know about us here. Call the cottage! Tell Platinum 7 to prepare for war!"

In the darkness of a deep hollow, five hundred metres inland from the cottage, Agent K crouched alongside a team of thirty MI5 officers. All of them wore protective combat gear.

Agent K's helmet contained a microphone and earpiece through which Queen Bee was relaying the news from London.

"Sirena is down and her cover is blown. They know we're on to them. Our only option is to launch the attack now. Maximum force! Go!"

"Logged," said Agent K. She flipped the microphone away. "Check body armour and weapons!" she shouted. "Go! Go! Go!"

The team sprang to their feet and quickly moved off. They spread out into two ranks, running towards the sound of waves crashing against the shore, keeping as low to the ground and as silent as they could. The moonlight bathed them in a faint blue glow and their breath misted in the cold night air as they levelled their machine guns.

The front door of the little cottage was suddenly flung open. Light from inside spilled out across the ground. The old man rushed out, carrying something large on his shoulder.

There was a booming whoosh, and a streak of vapour shot towards the oncoming MI5 agents. A rocket struck the grass ahead of them and the deafening explosion lit up the whole area in a flash. Half a dozen agents were knocked off their feet.

"Drop and return fire!" yelled Agent K.

The agents threw themselves to the ground. Streams of bullets spat from their machine guns, peppering the front of the cottage with small bursts of brick dust. Shards of glass flew from broken windows. The old man was hit many times, but he didn't so much as flinch. He fired again.

"Oh no, it's another android!" cried Agent K.

The second rocket exploded barely three metres from the front rank of agents. Agent K and two others were flung backwards. She landed on her back with a painful thud. Despite the ringing in her ears, she could hear a steady throb of power. The ground beneath her began to vibrate. Beyond the firing of the machine guns and the rocket explosions, she could see the shape of the offshore island changing.

It rose up, turning slowly. As it did so, hundreds of tonnes of earth and rock were shrugged off it, like a snake shedding its skin, revealing a long, sleek, silver aircraft driven by jets gushing blue flame from its underside. Splashes and waves surrounded it as the camouflage fell away. It continued to gain height, getting louder and louder as it did so.

Agent K struggled to stand as the MI5 agents around her continued lobbing grenades at the old man. One hit him on the shoulder. Before he could catch it and fling it aside, it detonated. The top half of the android was shredded into strips of plastic and metal, leaving its legs standing, the carpet slippers still on its feet.

"The base!" cried Agent K, as loudly as the pain in her chest would allow. "Bring it down! Bring it down!"

The agents turned their machine guns on the aircraft and aimed for the jets. But the base continued to rise, then banked swiftly to soar over the heads of its attackers.

At that moment, a beep sounded in Agent K's helmet. She flipped down her microphone.

"Hold your fire!" ordered Queen Bee in the laboratory at SWARM HQ. "I repeat, hold your fire!"

"What?" gasped Agent K, her voice scratchy over the damaged radio in her helmet.

"We've had new communications from the other SWARM agents," Queen Bee continued. "Sir Godfrey Kite and other civilians are on board that aircraft. Do not shoot it down! Do you copy?"

"Logged," said Agent K. "Cease fire!"

"Queen Bee out."

"Should we call for medical backup?" suggested Alfred Berners in a low voice.

"Agent K can take care of that," snapped Queen Bee. "She knows what she's doing." The stress of the situation was beginning to affect her in more ways than one. She took a deep breath then turned to Simon Turing and Professor Miller. "Anything from Sirena?"

Simon shook his head.

Professor Miller ran a nervous hand over his bald head. "All data streams show zero. Total deactivation is implied."

Queen Bee's expression was grim. "We can't bring down Silverclaw's base, Agent K and her men are in a bad way, we've lost track of the androids in London, and Sirena may have been destroyed. The Security Conference begins in just over eight hours' time. I don't think it's any exaggeration to say that the fate of the world rests with our micro-robots aboard that aircraft."

CHAPTER NINE

The morning rush hour was starting in central London. People were streaming in and out of tube stations, wrapped up against the chilly weather.

A few hundred metres from the Palace of Westminster, a stall had been set up. The side of a small van had been opened out and a man was selling coffee and tea. Now that his face had been fully repaired, Mercury 2 would not be detected by his many customers as anything other than a human salesperson.

Over a period of half an hour, four men and two women approached the stall when nobody else was queueing to be served. Each walked up to the stall and, without a word being exchanged, was given a large cup with a plastic lid. The final one, a man dressed in a smart business suit, was also handed a large rectangular briefcase. As soon as he had walked away, Mercury 2 closed up the van and drove off, disappearing into the dense traffic.

The last customer was Platinum 1, the android who had replaced Sir Godfrey Kite. After Gold Leader had given the androids new orders the night before, they had peeled away their faces and replaced them with completely different ones.

The six androids quietly made their way to a narrow alley behind a nearby restaurant. A rat scurried away as they approached. Pausing to check that they weren't being watched, they took the lids off their coffee cups. The cups were filled with clips of ammunition and the components of six handguns. Throwing the cups aside, they quickly assembled and loaded the guns. Once they'd hidden the weapons inside their clothes, they left the alley. Platinum 1 carried the heavy briefcase, containing enough high explosives to demolish half the Palace of Westminster.

A few streets away in Sir Godfrey Kite's flat, Agent J was talking to SWARM HQ.

"Yes, I've had the place locked down for hours," he said. "I'm the first person in here. There's no sign of the androids and no clue about where they might be now. I've got my armed police looking for them throughout the Palace of Westminster. They all have the androids' descriptions. There are orders to arrest 'Sir Godfrey' on sight, using any means necessary. He's the one with the highest level of access."

"Have you located Sirena?" said Queen Bee.

Agent J looked down into the palm of his hand. The robot butterfly lay twisted and motionless.

"I've run a quick scan with my phone," said Agent J. "There's electrical activity in her CPU, so I think her brain is functioning, but the damage is severe. Hercules or Nero might have survived, but..."

"Keep her safe and bring her back here as soon as you can," ordered Queen Bee.

"Logged," said Agent J. "I've heard that people are asking where Sir Godfrey is. He's expected to open the conference. We're putting out a cover story that he's ill, but it won't wash for long."

"Do your best," said Queen Bee. "In the meantime, keep your police team on full alert. Silverclaw know they're being watched."

"I'm going over to Westminster Hall right away," said Agent J.

Westminster Hall was the oldest part of the Palace of Westminster. It was a huge room, almost seventy-five metres long, with a wide stone staircase at one end. Its stone floor and walls were topped by a vaulted wooden roof. Way up, almost at roof level, elegantly arched windows ran along each side.

This was the venue for the World Leaders' Security Conference. The enormous hall echoed with the sounds of government staff, journalists and foreign officials preparing for the arrival of the sixty-seven delegates. In front of a bank of chairs, white cloths and small floral displays had been placed on a large, circular arrangement of tables. TV news teams were filming reports about the importance of the conference to world peace. Politicians talked with advisers and civil servants.

Agent J weaved his way through the hall, alert for any sign of the six androids. He was becoming increasingly nervous. There was less than half an hour before the first session of the conference. Silverclaw could strike at any moment.

An armed police officer came over to him. "Those other five on the list, sir – the two journalists, two Foreign Office staff and the cleaner."

"Yes?"

"No sign of any of them. They're not here, and they're not at their homes."

Agent J's gaze kept darting to the people around him. "They'll turn up, somehow," he said. "Every room's been re-scanned?"

"Twice. We've got men in the sewers,

helicopters in the air, marksmen on the roof, ID checks at every door."

"They know we're on to them," said Agent J. "They could try any number of ways to sneak in."

"Sir, we're practically inside a stone box," said the officer. "A bomb outside wouldn't work, the walls are too thick. They've got to get into this very room. And nobody's getting in here without being X-rayed, ID'd, filmed, questioned, logged and labelled."

Once the officer had returned to his duties, Agent J called Queen Bee at SWARM HQ.

"I don't get it," he said. "I've got CCTV and mobile units covering every millimetre of every street within half a mile. Those six androids can't get anywhere near the building without being recognized. Maybe they've decided not to strike today after all?"

"I might be prepared to believe that," said Queen Bee, "if it wasn't for the fact that our bugs are currently reporting the Silverclaw base as airborne. It's heading towards London at high altitude."

On board the Silverclaw base, the micro-robots were gathered behind the main control console at which Gold Leader was sitting. Hercules had cut three small, perfectly circular holes at different points along the base of the console. Nero and Morph were inside, sending fibre-optic probes into various circuits and components.

"Are you making progress?" said Chopper.

"Negative," said Nero. "There are lock-outs and coded sequences protecting every individual system."

"If we manage to crack the guidance controls," said Morph, "we'd still need to crack the power system, the central computer, the fuel regulators, the communications hub … everything."

"How long will it take to access the entire ship?" said Chopper.

"Even at maximum processing speed, a minimum of nine hours fourteen minutes," said Nero. "Plugging our own brains into key points in the computer grid would open up most systems, but there's a high risk of failure."

"What sort of high risk?" said Hercules.

"There is a 78.9 per cent probability that we would all be fused into lumps of metal and plastic," said Nero. "Not a successful end to our mission. Now that I've examined this ship's data streams I have discovered several things that may be of use to us. Firstly, there is an escape capsule located close to the cryonic section. It is only small, but we could use it to get the frozen humans to safety."

"If we can break into the cryonic controls," said Morph.

"Secondly," said Nero, "the androids being used in London require careful control. On this ship, two computers and three basic androids are used to monitor each one. Because of this complexity, introducing enough corrupted code into the androids' information feeds should enable us to shut them down permanently."

"If we can break into the transmission controls," said Morph.

"That might become top priority," said Chopper. "I've just contacted SWARM HQ.

Our mission objectives are to rescue the frozen humans, gain control of this base and capture Drake and Gold Leader. However Agent J and his security team are on full alert. There is no sign of the androids. The possibility of deactivating them from here needs to be investigated. Nero, that can be your job."

"Logged," said Nero. "I'll need to get inside the computer bank on the other side of this control room. Hercules, your assistance please."

Nero disconnected from the console and the two robots scuttled into the shadows.

"Widow, Morph, Sabre," said Chopper. "We need to find another way to access the rest of the ship's systems – and quickly."

"Where do we start?" said Morph.

Inside Westminster Hall, the first session of the Security Conference was under way. Britain's prime minister was addressing the seated delegates, in Sir Godfrey Kite's absence. Behind the delegates sat teams of officials. The prime minister welcomed the visitors and expressed the hope that the conference would be a turning point in the long road towards peace and the defeat of terrorism.

The entire area outside the Palace of Westminster was being closely monitored by a small army of MI5 agents, police and security guards. In nearby control centres, the footage from CCTV cameras was monitored and assessed by both humans and computers.

The six androids took no notice of anything the police were doing. One by one they walked calmly up St Margaret's Street until they were level with the area of lawn beside Westminster Hall.

As soon as they were all in position, they turned to face the Palace of Westminster.

Suddenly, miniature jet thrusters hidden inside their legs fired up. Like humanoid rockets, they shot up into the air, smoke and flames issuing from under their feet.

Yells and screams erupted all around. Agent J, keeping watch outside the hall, realized at once what was going on. He spun on his heels and ran back inside.

Shots rang out. Bullets ricocheted off the androids. Their flight paths remained straight and steady. With a series of almighty crashes, the six androids burst through the high windows near the roof of Westminster Hall, sending down showers of reinforced glass.

Once inside, the androids spun in mid-air and landed on the stone floor, their jet thrusters cutting out. All six drew their revolvers, grabbed the nearest human and held the guns to the terrified captives' heads.

"Stay where you are!" boomed Platinum 1. "If anyone attempts to leave, these humans will be shot. If anyone in this room attempts to disarm us, these humans will be shot."

The room was filled with gasps and angry cries. Platinum 1 placed the briefcase on the table in front of the British prime minister. He opened it to reveal the explosives packed tightly inside. Embedded in the centre of them was a timer with a large LED display. Platinum 1 entered a code into it, and it began a countdown.

10... 9...

The prime minister let out a loud yelp and hid under the table.

Agent J, who had run back into the hall just as the windows were shattering, opened an emergency channel on his smartphone.

"SWARM HQ," he whispered. "The team of bugs that met the helicopter at the airfield yesterday. Were both parts of their mission successful?"

"Confirmed," said Simon Turing at HQ.

4... 3... 2... 1...

Screams broke out across the hall.

Nothing happened.

Agent J shut his eyes for a second. "Well done, SWARM," he murmured to himself.

Back in the helicopter, SWARM had neutralized the danger by disabling every item in the consignment. Sabre had injected chemical pellets into the explosives to prevent them from detonating.

The six androids calmly took aim at their hostages and pulled the triggers. The guns clicked uselessly.

Platinum 1 brought down his fist on to the table in front of him and smashed it into splinters.

"The main strike must succeed," he said. "New orders needed. Requesting instructions."

Panic broke out and everyone began to race for the exit. One of the androids dug its hands into the nearest wall, scooped out a huge section of stone and flung it. The stone crashed against the exit, blocking it.

MI5 agents and police officers fired continuously at the androids, taking care not to injure their hostages, but the androids showed no reactions.

"HQ!" yelled Agent J into his smartphone. "Patch me through to the bugs on Silverclaw's base!"

Once Agent J was connected to the SWARM micro-robots, he yelled down the phone. "You've got to switch these androids off – now! We're trying to hold them back, but they're too strong. People could get killed any minute!"

"Logged," said Chopper. "Nero, Hercules, we need an update."

"I've tapped into the transmission controls," said Nero from inside a machine at the far end of the control room, "but they're all encrypted."

"Morph," said Chopper. "Have you found a bypass yet?"

"I think I've worked out a way to get around the problem," said Morph, "but it won't be easy."

"What is it?" said Chopper.

"Gold Leader's artificial arm contains an electronic key, which bypasses the security systems. To deactivate those androids in London, we've got to make her use it!"

CHAPTER TEN

Gold Leader was concentrating on the console in front of her, watching developments in London.

"Those weapons were useless!" she howled, watching data stream in from the six androids. "It's Drake again. He must have sabotaged those crates. I'll kill that scum-eating toad!"

An android at a nearby bank of controls turned its head towards her. "Platinum 1 to 6 awaiting orders," it said calmly.

"Cause as much destruction as they can!" she spat. "We'll land at the Palace of Westminster in a matter of minutes. By then I want every living thing in Westminster Hall wiped out!"

"Acknowledged," said the android.

Morph scuttled across the floor and around Gold Leader's mechanical leg. He flattened his gelatinous body and squeezed through the tiny gap between two small metal plates in her heel. Quickly, he plugged himself into the signals running Gold Leader's implants.

"Let's see now…" he said.

Suddenly, Gold Leader's artificial arm jerked. She looked at it in alarm. It twisted and reached out towards the console in front of her.

"W-what's going on?" she cried.

Her mechanical hand opened up with a click and a whirr. The security key inside it sprang forward. The arm jerked again, fixing the electronic key into a connector on the console and turning it ninety degrees.

"What the…?" yelled Gold Leader.

A series of beeps sounded. "Transmission system opened," said one of the nearby androids.

"I have access!" said Nero, deep inside the electronics at the other end of the room. "Uploading viral decryption program now!"

In Westminster Hall, the six androids were fighting against the teams of police officers and secret service agents. Platinum 1 had a crushing hand around Agent J's throat and was raising him off his feet. Agent J's legs kicked and wheeled.

Suddenly, the androids emitted a high-pitched burst of static. For a moment, they froze. Platinum 1 let go of Agent J and the SWARM agent dropped to the stone floor, spluttering.

The small crowd of conference delegates and officials stared at the androids, open-mouthed. The androids slumped and twitched, their faces sliding as the electronics behind them began to burn out. An eyeball fell from Platinum 1's head. All six crumpled to their knees, then fell sideways as wisps of smoke began to rise from their joints.

Morph was tapping into every signal he could find. He made Gold Leader spin round and march across the control room.

"Stop! What's happening?" she snarled. "How did the Platinum units fail? How?"

Her artificial arm twirled in a circle around her head, and her leg suddenly sent her stepping forwards and backwards, forwards and backwards. She shrieked in alarm and wrestled her mechanical arm with her human one, twisting and struggling.

"It's surprisingly difficult to coordinate it all," said Morph.

He jerked her arm to one side, and plugged the arm's electronic key into a succession of connections along the front of a computer bank. Lights above each connection switched from red to green, and beeps sounded across the control room.

"Power system opened…" said an android. "Cryonic system opened… Fuel system opened…"

"Don't just stand there!" yelled Gold Leader. "Stop me!"

Two androids calmly walked over to her and grasped her by her shoulders. They carried her back to the main control console, her implants jittering and whirling all the way.

"Have we got into everything yet?" said Hercules.

"All except the flight guidance controls," said Morph. "I'm getting the hang of this, I'll get her to unlock those right now."

Struggling angrily, Gold Leader used her human arm to reach across and break off the electronic key. She dashed it to the floor and it smashed to pieces.

"Oh," said Morph. "Too late."

"At least the cryonic system is open," said Chopper. "Sabre, free the human prisoners and get them into the escape capsule."

"Logged," said Sabre. He buzzed along the control-room ceiling and headed off down the corridor.

Morph disconnected from the circuits inside Gold Leader's mechanical leg and squeezed back out on to the floor of the control room. Gold Leader sat in her chair, opening panels on her artificial arm and examining its components.

"What the devil is going on?" she muttered.

She turned to the nearest android. "How many Mercury units are on board?"

"Twenty-nine are currently operating," said the android. "A further thirty-four are ready to be powered up."

"Enough," nodded Gold Leader. "We'll land them at Westminster. We're only minutes away, so the delegates won't have had time to disperse. Arm all units with whatever we've got that works. We're not beaten yet!"

"Acknowledged," said the android.

Morph scuttled back to Widow, Hercules and Chopper behind the control console. Nero uploaded a few more lines of code into the ship's computer, to prevent Gold Leader from regaining control of the systems that had been unlocked, then joined the others.

"Once the human prisoners are freed," said Chopper, "we have to take over the flight controls. This base still poses a significant threat to human life. We'll have to resort to Nero's alternative solution."

"The one where we're likely to be fried to a crisp?" said Hercules.

"Affirmative," said Chopper.

"I was hoping you wouldn't say that," said Morph.

Gold Leader clutched her mechanical arm and sat in silence for a moment. The human sections of her face were awash with fear and anger. "Something's worming its way through my ship."

At that moment, the control console bleeped. "All pods in cryonic storage section have been opened," said an android monitoring computer readouts.

Gold Leader leaped to her feet. "Drake!"

Seven humans were blinking and rubbing their eyes as they stepped out of the cryonic sleeping pods. They stared at their surroundings, unable to understand where they were.

"What's going on?" mumbled the real Sir Godfrey Kite. "Last thing I remember was … my office…"

Sabre tapped into the base's communications

circuits. His amplified voice echoed from a speaker set into the ceiling. "There is an escape capsule to your right. Please get into it as quickly as possible. I am an agent of the British secret service. You'll be taken to safety."

"Who is that?" said Sir Godfrey. "Where are you?"

"Please hurry," said Sabre.

Drake swayed groggily for a few moments, then pushed past the six others. "Get out of my way! I'm taking it!"

He stabbed the button beside the hatch leading into the escape capsule. The hatch opened with a hiss of air. Before Drake could step inside, Sabre zipped down from the ceiling and injected a pellet into his leg.

"Yahhh!" screeched Drake. He collapsed to the floor, clutching his calves.

"Freezer sting delivered," said Sabre.

The others, still dazed and confused, crammed themselves into the small capsule.

"The capsule is designed to be piloted," transmitted Sabre to the other bugs. "There are too many people in it for efficient operation, and none of them are likely to have the skills to operate it anyway. I will go with them and pilot the capsule by remote control."

"Logged," said Chopper.

Drake yelped as he tried and failed to stand up. The people in the capsule were too groggy to notice a mosquito landing just inside the hatch. The escape capsule closed and a transparent bulkhead sealed the capsule off from the rest of the base.

Drake banged on the bulkhead as he watched the capsule slip away and out into the open air. "No! Come back!"

A hand suddenly seized him from behind.

"Let them go," said Gold Leader. "They're no use to me now ... but you are!"

Drake found himself dragged along the shiny floor of the corridor that led back to the control room.

"What did you bring on board my ship, Drake?" demanded Gold Leader. "A computer virus? Some sort of electronic gadget made by MI5?"

"Let go! I don't know what you're talking about!"

"Everything's started to go wrong since you got here! Coincidence?"

"Yes!" He could feel the effects of Sabre's sting wearing off. His legs were a mass of pins and needles.

Gold Leader dragged him into the control room. All the androids working at consoles and computers were now armed with pistols. "You just tried to escape. What more proof do I need that you're a traitor? I was going to hand you over to our masters, but now that the main strike has been sabotaged, I'm taking desperate measures. I'm going to be in trouble for allowing the Silverclaw operation to be jeopardized, so I'm going to get back in their favour by killing the MI5 spy who made everything go wrong!"

She pulled a lever and a circular section of the floor slid back. There was a howling rush of cold air. Drake could see the outskirts of London, thousands of metres below.

"People say you die of shock before you hit the ground," cried Gold Leader, her hair thrashing wildly in the wind. "Let's see if they're right."

"No!" shouted Drake. Gold Leader hauled him

towards the opening in the floor. He wriggled and clawed.

The micro-robots were powerless to help him. They had taken up their positions inside the control room's guidance circuits.

"At our current speed, we are one hundred and thirty-two seconds from the Palace of Westminster," said Nero.

"Prepare for power build-up," said Chopper.

"I hope this isn't going to hurt," said Morph.

"If this doesn't work," said Hercules, "we'll be too busy blowing up to care whether it hurts or not."

"That's not at all reassuring," said Morph.

"We have to store as much of the ship's output in our own capacitors as we can," said Nero. "Then we channel a surge of power through the guidance system to force it to reboot. If we're not smears of charcoal, we can then take over the flight controls before the computer knows what's happening."

Drake was rapidly regaining the use of his legs. He struggled to free himself from Gold Leader's grip. They grappled across the floor of the control room, the outside air swirling around them. The androids, having no orders to move, stayed calmly at their posts.

"Power building," said Chopper. "500 kilowatts stored... 600 ... 700..."

"We are one hundred and eight seconds from the Palace of Westminster," said Nero.

Drake suddenly aimed a kick at the nearest android and knocked its pistol to the floor. Wrenching himself to one side with a yell, Drake dived for the gun.

Gold Leader flung herself at him. Drake snatched up the gun and fired a volley of bullets. The impact sent Gold Leader flying back, screaming. She dropped to the floor, her mechanical limbs sparking. Her whole body became engulfed in blue arcs of electricity. For a moment she grasped at the air, then fell motionless.

Drake flung the gun aside. "She was right," he gasped. "Our masters are never going to believe me. I've got to destroy that conference or I'm a dead man." He turned to the android beside him. "Decrease altitude! Increase speed! We'll land directly outside the Palace of Westminster and launch an all-out attack!"

"We are not programmed to respond to unauthorized personnel," replied the android calmly.

"Speed increasing," said Nero. "59 seconds to impact."

The bugs began to overheat as their brains soaked up the output of the ship's computers.

"Holding 2 megawatts..." said Hercules. "2.2 ... 2.4..."

"Prepare to send power surge!" said Chopper.

"We can't!" cried Morph. "It's too much!"

"47 seconds..." said Nero.

Drake stood close to the hole in the floor, holding on to one of the control consoles to steady himself. The base shook as it flew faster and faster.

Behind him, a smoking artificial hand groped for the gun he'd dropped. Above the howl of the wind, he couldn't hear Gold Leader cry, "Traitor!"

In her last second of life, she pulled the trigger. Drake lurched and spun, an expression of horrified surprise on his face. He was dead before he hit the ground.

"29 seconds..." said Nero.

"Now!" said Chopper.

Together, the micro-robots reversed the flow of power through their circuits. The surge ripped through their brains like forks of lightning. All five of them felt their electronic components begin to smoke and crack.

The whole aircraft bucked and shook.

"Flight controls ... rebooting?" said Chopper weakly.

"22 seconds to impact..." said Nero.

At that moment, lights began to flicker on the control room's main console. One by one they blinked red, yellow, green.

"Navigation online!" said Hercules.

"Steer us clear! Quick!" gasped Morph.

"Internal power ... going..." said Chopper.

On Westminster Bridge, beside the Palace of Westminster, people watched in horror as a huge sleek silver shape shot towards them.

The Silverclaw base was out of control, racing along above the waters of the Thames, heading directly for the tower of Big Ben.

Screams broke out as it got closer and closer. People ducked for cover and braced themselves for an explosion.

At the last second, the aircraft turned in mid-air. It twisted and shot vertically upwards. Then it banked, slowed down, and dropped heavily into the murky waters of the Thames, sending huge waves crashing against the banks.

From all around came the sound of emergency sirens.

CHAPTER ELEVEN

Several days later, a meeting involving all the SWARM agents was held at SWARM HQ. Agent K had her arm in a sling and Sirena was still damaged, but she was able to take her place on the workbench alongside the others.

Agent J made his report to Queen Bee. "It took me quite a while to cut the five of them loose from inside that computer. Their power cells had been almost fried by the power surge that got them control of the ship. Once they were safely retrieved, I let the police tow away the wreck and recover the dead bodies of Morris Drake and

Alexis Vendetti."

Queen Bee turned to the bugs. "How are you all feeling?"

"Mechanical and electrical systems are at ninety-two per cent efficiency," said Nero.

"My circuits are still stinging," grumbled Morph quietly.

"Fortunately," said Professor Miller, "I was able to replace their burnt-out components without having to completely disassemble them, but it was a close shave. A few more seconds at that kind of power level and they'd have been destroyed. The damage to Sirena was mostly mechanical. I'm working on a new pair of wings made from a similar gelatinous material to Morph's exoskeleton."

"I'll be able to wrap my wings around myself for protection," said Sirena.

"Well," said Queen Bee, "you all risked a great deal and did a superb job."

"Although none of us can take any official credit for foiling the Silverclaw plot," said Simon Turing.

"That's the price of having to remain top secret," smiled Alfred Berners.

"There is still one mystery," said Hercules. "Who were Drake and Gold Leader really working for? Who were the masters they were so afraid of?"

"Whoever they are," said Queen Bee, "let's hope that this defeat makes them think twice. For the moment, we can celebrate another successful mission for SWARM!"

In a low, concrete room, a very long way from London, another meeting was in progress. Around a heavy wooden table sat nine people.

At the head of a table was their commander. "Now that The Nine are assembled," he said in a slow, whispering voice, "we can assess the damage done to our plans." He pushed gently at a few sheets of paper that were set out on the table in front of him. "It seems clear that there is a hidden department in the British secret service that has been directly responsible for ruining several carefully organized operations. The Silverclaw project has been defeated and our agents Vendetti and Drake are dead."

The others murmured respectfully.

"The Firestorm project was defeated. The New Age project was defeated. Our acquisition of the deadly toxin known as Venom was only possible at the last moment, because we had Drake inside MI5 at the time."

The others nodded.

"This hidden department has caused us trouble for the last time. It is to be put out of action, permanently."

HAVE YOU READ?

**A top-secret device with the power
to bring down the world's electronic
communications has been stolen.**

**It's a race against time for SWARM to locate
and retrieve the dangerous weapon before the
thieves crack the encryption code protecting
it. Can the SWARM team stop the villains
before it's too late?**

Turn the page to read an extract...

CHAPTER ONE

"Queen Bee to agents! Prepare to move out!"

Two electronic voices replied, one after the other. "I'm live, Queen Bee."

Queen Bee sat in a high-backed black leather chair, in front of a wide bank of brightly lit screens and readouts. She was a tall woman with a shock of blonde hair and a smartly cut suit. She wore a pair of glasses with small, circular lenses that reflected the rapidly shifting light from the screens. Behind the lenses, her steely grey eyes darted from one readout to another, soaking up information. Her age was difficult to work out from her looks, but her slightly pursed lips, and the way her long fingers tapped slowly on the arms of her chair, showed that she meant business.

One of the screens in front of her showed a man coming out of an office block. Numbers and graphs danced across the lower part of the image, sensor readings of everything from the air temperature at his location to his current heart rate.

Queen Bee leaned forward and spoke into a microphone, which jutted out on a long, flexible stalk. "Chopper, begin data recording."

"Logged, Queen Bee," said one of the electronic voices. It had a slightly lower tone than the other one.

Outside the office block, Marcus Oliphant sniffed at the morning breeze for a moment. He was a tall, stringy man with bushy eyebrows and a loping walk. His nose wrinkled. The smell of vehicle exhaust seemed stronger than usual today. He took a tighter grip of the small metal case he was carrying, then set off along the street. The traffic of central London rumbled and roared past.

A long set of black-painted railings ran alongside him. He didn't notice two insects perched on top. One was a tiny mosquito, the other a large, iridescent dragonfly. At least, that's what they appeared to be. They didn't jump and flit like insects usually do. Instead, they seemed to be watching him.

As he walked off down the road, the insects' wings buzzed into life, and they rose into the air, following him at a short distance.

As the insects rose, so the image on the screen in front of Queen Bee shifted and moved.

Queen Bee swung around in her chair. Sitting behind her were half a dozen people with serious, quizzical expressions on their faces. Among them were the Home Secretary, the head of MI5 and Queen Bee's boss, the leader of the UK's Secret Intelligence Agency.

"As you can see, ladies and gentlemen," said

Queen Bee, "the subject has no idea that he's being tailed. Our micro-robots are much more effective than normal secret service agents, with their blindingly obvious dark glasses and their suspiciously unmarked fast cars."

The head of MI5 shuffled grumpily in his seat. "And much more expensive. How much are these technological toy soldiers costing, Home Secretary? You gave the SIA the go-ahead for this programme."

The Home Secretary looked slightly uncomfortable. "A lot. I'm afraid I don't have the figures to hand," she muttered.

"The latest technology is never cheap," said Queen Bee. "But my section, the Department of Micro-robotic Intelligence, has capabilities that make it priceless. The existence of SWARM is known only to my staff, and to the people in this room. However, nanotechnology is the future. Micro-robots will soon dominate the worlds of spying and crime investigation. These SWARM operatives are the most advanced robots on Earth. On the outside, they are almost indistinguishable from real insects, yet each has equipment and capabilities that make the average undercover agent look like a caveman."

The Home Secretary pointed to the screen. "Who is that man? What's this demonstration supposed to prove?"

"He's Marcus Oliphant, leader of the team that's developed the new Whiplash weapon," said Queen Bee. "It has been created by a private company, Techna-Stik International, and is being sold to the British government. The prototype is in that metal case there – it's only the size of a matchbox. He's on his way to meet with your own officials, Home Secretary, and show them the progress that's been made. I've asked for my robots to shadow him today, to show their effectiveness. Normally, an MI5 operative would be assigned, but since Whiplash is every bit as secret as SWARM, this man's visit has been judged low risk. No unauthorized person could possibly know what he's carrying."

"Whiplash?" said the Home Secretary. "Have I been briefed on that?" She turned to the man beside her.

"It's an EMP device," said the head of MI5.

"Extremely dangerous in the wrong hands."

"Extremely dangerous even in the right hands," muttered Queen Bee.

"EMP?" frowned the Home Secretary.

"Electro-magnetic pulse," explained Queen Bee. "It emits an invisible wave of energy which knocks out all electrical circuits. Fries them beyond repair. It does almost no physical damage, but destroys electronics – everything from air-traffic control to TV remotes. Vehicles, computers, the lot, all made useless."

"Whiplash shoots a narrow EMP beam across a few kilometres," said the head of MI5. "It's designed to target and disable enemy systems."

Suddenly, the high electronic voice of the mosquito cut across the air. "Sabre to Queen Bee. Suspicious activity detected."

Queen Bee leaned forward and spoke into the microphone. "Specify."

Out on the street, Chopper the robotic dragonfly whipped around in mid-air to direct his high-definition cameras towards a vehicle approaching from behind. His eyes zoomed in to reveal a powerful, dark blue BMW that was slowing down, causing cars behind it to overtake.

Chopper transmitted the data back to Queen Bee at SWARM headquarters. "The registration number does not match the car type listed on the national database," he said. "Stolen car, I think. Or stolen licence plates."

"Can you get a look at the driver?" radioed Queen Bee.

Chopper adjusted the thermal imaging in his eyes. "Negative, Queen Bee, too many reflections off the glass."

"Sabre," said Queen Bee, "stay close to the target."

"Logged," replied the mosquito. He buzzed closer to Oliphant, the man with the metal case, who took a casual swat at his shoulder.

Suddenly, the BMW roared ahead. Swerving violently, it bounced up on to the pavement in front of Oliphant, its brakes squealing. The doors were flung open and four men wearing balaclavas jumped out.

Oliphant stood open-mouthed, too alarmed to run. The man who'd been driving grabbed the metal case and knocked Oliphant flying with a sharp punch.

"Attack mode," said Chopper calmly. "Target compromised."

A tiny, needle-like proboscis flicked forward from Sabre's head. He dived swiftly towards the driver and stabbed at the man's neck in a lightning movement.

"Oww!" yelled the driver. "What was—?" Then he twitched, wide-eyed, dropped the metal case and toppled forward on to the pavement.

"Freezer sting delivered," said Sabre.

The other three men hauled the driver to his feet, grabbed the case and quickly got back into the BMW. Chopper circled, recording every detail of the attackers and their car. Oliphant sat on the pavement, dazed and rubbing his jaw.

The car lurched into life, roared around in a U-turn and sprang back on to the road. An approaching bus braked hard to avoid a collision and blasted its horn at the BMW. A small group of pedestrians were gathering around Oliphant, offering help. One was already calling the police on his mobile.

"The human is receiving assistance," said Chopper. "Pursue the weapon."

Chopper and Sabre swung round and darted off down the street after the BMW.

Queen Bee's voice buzzed in the insects' receivers. "Get to that car! Sabre, inject a tracker into one of those men!"

"Logged," said Sabre.

Chopper's vision zoomed in on the car as it raced ahead. "Windows closed. No entry. We may be able to gain access through an air vent."

Both insect robots flew at maximum speed. Chopper the dragonfly was larger and faster through the air than Sabre the mosquito, but even he struggled to keep up with the BMW. The car was weaving through the traffic, honking other vehicles out of the way and shifting up a gear.

"Personal speed limits reached," said Chopper. "The car's too fast for us. We will lose it in 19.4 seconds."

"Suggestion," piped up Sabre. "I can inject a

micro-explosive into one of the car's tyres. That will force it to stop."

Chopper paused, his miniature circuits making complex calculations. "Chance of success on a moving vehicle is only nine per cent. That action is not advised."

Sabre computed the information. "Your advice is ignored. I'm going to attempt it. The mission comes first. Our orders were to safeguard Whiplash, so now we must recover it."

**Read *OPERATION STING*
to find out what happens next!**

SIMON CHESHIRE

Simon is the award-winning author of the
Saxby Smart and *Jeremy Brown* series.
Simon's ultimate dream is to go to the moon,
but in the meantime, he lives in Warwick
with his wife and children. He writes in a
tiny room, not much bigger than a wardrobe,
which is crammed with books, pieces of
paper and empty chocolate bar wrappers.
His hobbies include fixing old computers
and wishing he had more hobbies.

www.simoncheshire.co.uk